'Funny yet Shocking!'

A SCREENELLA BY WRITER, DIRECTOR

Sithesh C Govind

INDIA • SINGAPORE • MALAYSIA

ISBN 979-8-89026-361-2

This work is purely fictional, Characters and events, entirely fictional, any resemblance to real-life incidents or persons, is coincidental and not intended as versions. The author's views don't align with characters' deeds, the story's content, the author doesn't endorse or heed, it's an imaginary tale that aims to entertain, and any connection to reality is purely inane.

Contents

About the Author

Sithesh C Govind is a film director, screenwriter, and advertising professional who works as the creative director for leading ad agencies and film productions, His debut feature film in Kannada, "Idu Entha Lokavayya," was nominated for the 13th Bengaluru International Film Festival (Biffes 2022). He lives with 3 lovely females;), his wife Deepa, a creative contributor-writer, and two lovely daughters, Dia and Nia.

Connect with Sithesh C Govind

Visit www.CreativeDirector.in *or* www.SitheshCGovind.com

Email him at sithesh@gmail.com

Find him on Facebook at www.Facebook.com/SitheshCGovind

Follow him on Instagram at @creativedirector.in

Explore his IMDb page at SitheshCGovind

Acknowledgements

If I had to begin expressing my gratitude, I'd have to list out names of hundreds of amazing people in my life, who supported, guided and criticised me throughout my life until now.

I dedicate this book to my father Govind, mother Chandra Lehkha Govind, and brother Sineesh C Govind, who have shown me unconditional love and support throughout my life.

I've been working on this story idea based on Deepa Sithesh's one-liner, which we had previously discussed. She deserves my heartfelt thanks for being a constant source of encouragement and valuable inputs during my writing process.

I would like to express my heartfelt gratitude and appreciation to Kling Johnson for his invaluable assistance in structural editing with precision and accuracy, and for his unwavering support until the publication.

I am grateful to Benz Peter for his valuable insights and quick assistance during the initial draft of my work, as well as his continued support throughout the process.

My sincere appreciation goes out to the countless talented actors and actresses who have left a lasting impression on me with their remarkable performances in various languages.

I would like to express my heartfelt thanks to the incredible actors JayaSurya, Vinay Forrt and Fahadh Faasil for their inspiration to write this story.

Meanwhile, I also convey my heartfelt thanks to Naresh Pishorody and Madhav Das for their feedback on my first draft.

Thank you to my sweet daughters Dia and Nia for volunteering their time to illustrate Dada's book cover page.

I want to thank Notion Press for supporting my book's publication and for their assistance.

I appreciate all of my followers on social media, as well as the well-wishers and friends who continue to support me. Thank you so much to everyone who opts to read this book.

For all of your priceless assistance in making this book come to life.

And for that, I will always be grateful and humbled. I appreciate each and every one of you.

– Sithesh C Govind

When I narrated the plot of this story to National Award Winner Malayalam actor Jayasurya, he responded, "We've never heard of anything like this; this is an interesting plot; you should develop this idea. This is something funny yet shocking." Thank you to actor Jayasurya for providing the drive to finish this book.

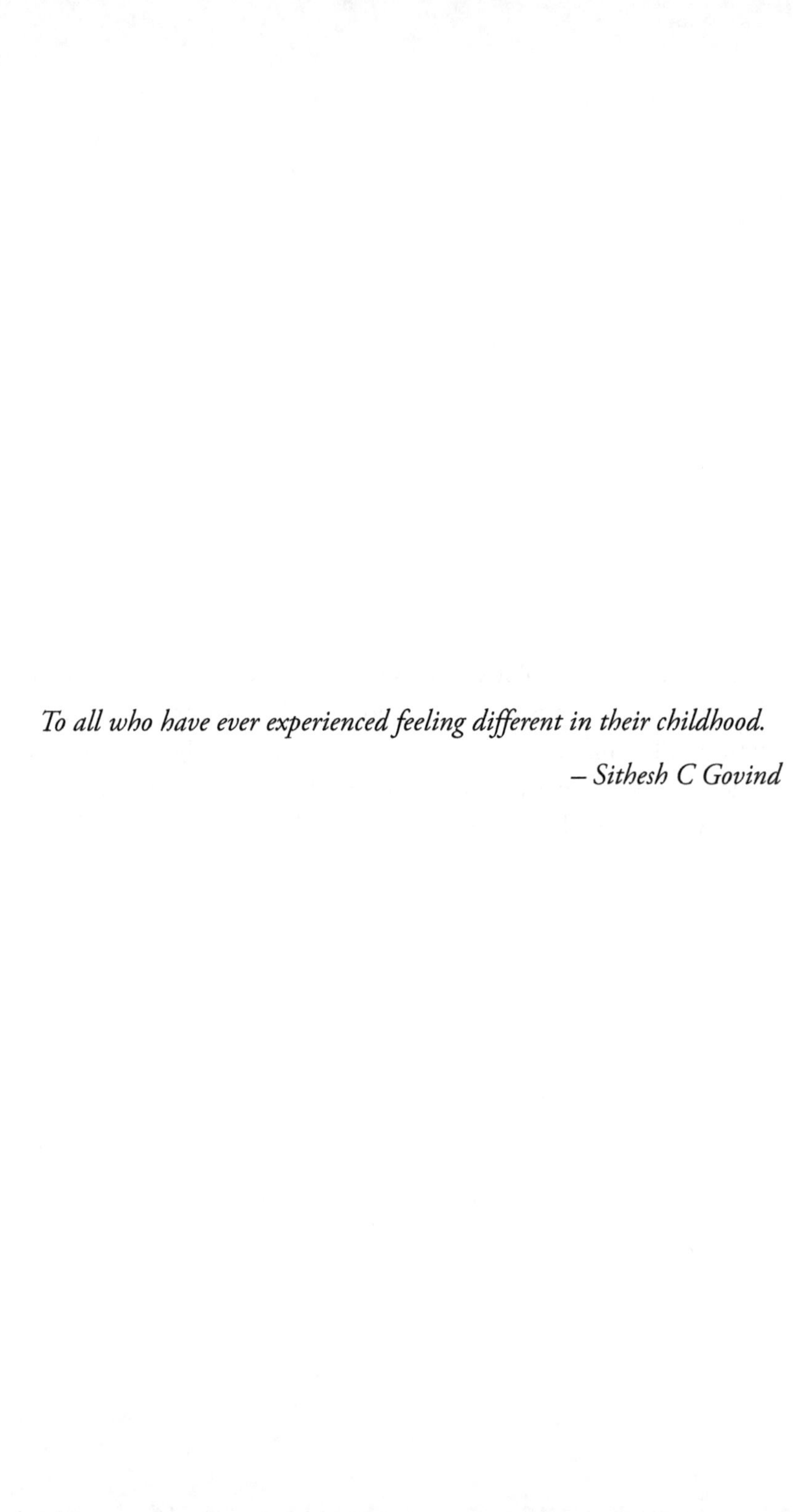

To all who have ever experienced feeling different in their childhood.

– Sithesh C Govind

Characters

1. Manojan - *Protagonist*
2. Vijayan - *Manojan's father*
3. Sumitramma - *Manojan's mother*
4. Ashwathi - *Manojan's elder sister*
5. Shinoj - *Manojans brother in-law, Ashwathi's husband*
6. Prasoon - *Manojan's niece*
7. Prabhi - *Manojan's niece*
8. Maalu - *Manojan's younger sister*
9. Girish - *Manojans Brother in-law, Maalu's husband*
10. Maalus Kid - *Manojan's niece*
11. Chekkutty Chettan - *Shopkeeper*
12. Purushan - *Who hates manojan*
13. Diljit - *Purushan's son*
14. Surabhi - *Manojan's life partner*
15. Sumesh - *Manojan's friend*
16. Suja - *Sumesh's wife*
17. Sonumon - *Sumesh's son*
18. Dr. Shanawas - *Manojan & Surabhi's Doctor*
19. Dr. Shifali - *Manojan & Surabhi's Doctor*

20. S.I. Jnansheelan - *Town S.I*

21. Kunjipalan - *Panchayat President*

22. Prafullan - *Local area Secretary*

23. William Lawyer - *Shrewd Lawyer*

24. Wilson Lawyer - *William Layers Son*

25. Babu - *Manojan's Assistant*

26. Lady-1 - *Cashew factory worker*

27. Lady-2 - *Cashew factory worker*

28. Smijoy - *Diljith's Friend*

29. Shiju - *Smijoy's Friend*

30. Magistrate - *Town Court Judge*

31. Sugunan - *Bus Traveller*

32. Sukumaran- *Medical representative*

33. Shobana Ettathi - *Sumithramma's assistant cook*

34. Bindu - *Manojan's prospective bride*

35. Bindus Uncle

36. Susamma - *Biology Teacher*

37. Raji Teacher

38. Lawyer's Assistant

39. Court employees

40. Gangettan

41. Police 1 & 2

42. Headmaster

43. ICU Doctor

Locations

Northern Kerala and nearby places, Cheriyandi Plakkal House, Magistrate Court, Govt. Hospital, Police Station, School, Kollur, Coorg, Mangalore, Bakel fort.

The storytelling style in this book is unique and one-of-a-kind. It combines a novella's narrative with the technical structure of a screenplay. I've named this genre Screenella, invented and practiced by me as an experiment in my writing process and proud to introduce it as a new publishing genre.

Presenting the first ever Screenella to you all. "A Nutty Affair," I hope you will all enjoy it. Thank you.

– Sithesh C Govind

As you read, imagine your favourite actor and actress in it.

A Nutty Affair

A Screenella by Sithesh C Govind

CHAPTER 1

The Mangaluru-Kasargod Route

Fade In

Day/Int./Ext.

The camera begins with an establishing shot of the Mangaluru State Bank Private Bus Stand, with the bustling activity of buses and people in the background. As the shot zooms in, a green and red-painted private bus comes into view, driving along a busy road.

The camera then switches to an interior shot of the bus, where passengers are seen sitting in their seats, some chatting with their neighbours while others are lost in their own thoughts.

Cutting back to an exterior shot, the camera follows the bus as it travels along the road, passing by various landmarks on its way to Kasaragod. The bright sunlight of the day illuminates the landscape around the bus, with green trees and fields stretching out in all directions.

As the bus approaches the border between Karnataka and Kerala, the camera focuses on the Chandragiri River, also known as the Payaswini River. It originates in Karnataka's Patti Ghat Hills, in a reserve forest of the Coorg district, with its clear waters flowing beneath the bridge. The river serves as a symbolic divide between two distinct regions, Tulunadu and the Malayalam-speaking regions, and the camera captures the majesty of the river as it winds its way through the lush landscape.

The camera pans to the right, revealing the impressive Chandragiri Fort in the distance. The fort is visible as the bus passes by, giving passengers a taste of the region's rich cultural and historical heritage. Overall, the camera positions in this scene capture the beauty and diversity of the landscape as well as the cultural and historical significance of the journey.

The camera pans to the back of the driver's seat, where a vibrant and colourful music player is uphung, playing the famous Kannada song "Jothe jotheyali iruvenu heege endu" from the movie of the renowned Kannada actor, Shankar Nag. Shankar Nag's headshot sticker is prominently displayed on the back of the driver's seat, paying homage to the legendary actor.

The camera shows a glimpse of the middle row of the bus, where Manojan, a 38-year-old man, is sitting comfortably with a relaxed expression on his face. He appears to be enjoying the Kannada song playing in the background as he hums along to the tune. The camera then zooms in to focus on Manojan, highlighting his features and showcasing his distinctive personality. As the camera lingers on him, it becomes clear that Manojan is the protagonist of the story, and his introduction sets the tone for the narrative to follow.

Manojan is watching out the window to his right while sharing a seat with an elderly passenger who is also looking out the window. A middle-aged man, Sugunan, enters the bus with his two kids, a girl who is seven and a boy who is five. While pulling both of his kids by their hands, he moves toward the center of the bus. Sugunan, who is from the same town as Manjonan, starts talking.

Sugunan: Hello Manojan, have you been to Mangalore?

Manojan: Yeah, I went there to buy a new sofa for decoration purposes. At Mangaluru…

As Manojan continued, Sugunan was busy searching for seats for his children. Manojan paused with a blink while Sugunan instructed his children to sit on Manojan's lap, curving up his eyebrow.

Sugunan: Sunikutta, Go and sit on Uncle's lap.

While the children move towards him, Manojan immediately gets up from his seat, even without looking at their faces.

Manojan: It's ok Sugunetta, you can occupy my seat, and anyway I am getting down at the next stop 'kavala market'.

The camera captures a wide shot of the bus as it approaches the bustling market crossroads. The lens used in this shot is a wide-angle lens, which provides a broader perspective and captures more of the scene.

As the bus slows down to a stop, the camera zooms in for a mid-shot of Manojan as he stands up, ready to disembark. His expression is calm and collected, revealing a sense of confidence and purpose. The lens used for this shot is a medium lens, which provides a more focused view of the subject.

The camera then transitions to a tracking shot as Manojan walks towards the back of the bus, showing the other passengers who are still seated. The camera follows Manojan as he steps off the bus.

The scene dissolves to a long shot of the bus as it moves forward, leaving Manojan behind at the market crossroads. The lens used for this shot is a long lens, which captures a distant view and emphasizes the distance between Manojan and the bus.

Dissolve to

CHAPTER 2

The Large Bronze Spatula

Day/Int./Ext.

The scene opens with a wide shot of the exterior of the old store. The camera then zooms in on Manojan as he walks towards the entrance of Chekutty Chettan's store, which sells large cooking utensils, copper vessels, large ladles, and spoons used at weddings. He can vaguely hear the Akashvani Mangaluru broadcast from an old radio as he enters.

As he explores around, stroking with his knuckle on the large bronze vessels, he grabs a metal spatula and turns towards Chekutty Chettan

Manojan: Chetta, The brass spatula these days isn't strong like before, but doesn't lack lustre.

Chekutty Chettan: You put it down there, and try this, it's strong and also lacks the luster you desire.

Chekutichettan points toward the side of the large biryani bowls kept aside. Manojan turns to find various types of large spatulas, paltas, and kitchen shovels. Manojan pulls out a 5-foot-long biryani shovel from the lot.

Manojan: Yes, I'm taking this longer one... Chekutty Chetta.

By that time, another customer and his family walked into the shop. Manojan paid off the money and walked away from the shop with a long shove in his hand.

Cut to

It was a hot early afternoon, and Manojan kept walking with the shovel through the market's narrow path that connects to the main road, arriving at the main road and standing in front of Dr. Kailasanathan's old dispensary, looking towards the end of the road as if he were expecting someone.

A 42-year-old man Purushan walks out of the dispensary with his five-month-pregnant wife and their three children: Diljith, ten, and two younger sisters. Purushan has a large cover of medical scan reports and some plastic covers in his hand. Purushan looks at Manojan and asks

What is this Manoja? Why are you standing here with this shovel in your hand?

While Purushan gestures to his wife and children to move back from the road and tells Manojan

Purushan: Good to see you here, I was about to tell you when you would come to my shop. In the last lot of cashew nut packets that you delivered, some of the nuts were more yellowish in colour than usual.

Manojan: Oh, those packets... Export quality cashews grades are like that, it's more yellowish hue.

Purushan: Whatever... Manoja, this month 19th is my daughter's birthday, so we decided to arrange a party, a small program, that's all. You need to take care of everything, some decorative string lights, and balloons are a must, and a dinner for 40 people with rice, vegetables, Sambar and add-ons. Let there be a small ice cream also, and let the children be happy.

After hearing this, Manojan asks sluggishly while glancing at the two kids who are standing next to Purushan's wife.

Manojan: Purushetta, see! Is it necessary to hold such lavish birthday parties for kids?

Manojan looks down at Purushan's wife's swollen stomach

Manojan: That too...... at this time

Purushan: You think only I want it? She is longing to celebrate too... Look, if you can't do it, let me know, I will ask Vijayettan to arrange everything.

Hearing that, Manojan tries to get rid of Purushu by showing some haste and tells him

Manojan: Then you ask him to do it. That would be better. I'm a little busy right now.

Realizing that Manojan is not interested, Purushan feels dejected goes to his wife, and tells her

Purushan: He is ever ready to immediately erect a pandal for free if anyone dies in town but has never ever got time to arrange a children's program.

Murmuring his words, Purushan spoke.

Huh! It's useless to try to explain about children to him; he'll never understand.

Purushan looks at his pregnant wife with a smile, and she beams.

Dissolve In

CHAPTER 3

It's the Mating Season!

Day/Ext.

It's quite sunny outside. As the camera pans out, we see Manojan standing in front of the clinic with the shovel in his hand when his friend Sumesh, who is around 35 years old, comes on the scooter and abruptly stops beside him.

Sumesh: Am I late....when you called from the bus stand, we hadn't even left town, and then I dropped Suja off at home...

Sumesh tells Manojan to board the scooter. Manojan while lifting the shovel asks Sumesh

Did you meet Purushan while coming?

Sumesh: No.

Manojan: He was with his wife at the Kailasanathan's clinic for a checkup and left just now. I just don't get it; is this a mating season, just like wedding season?

Sumesh throws a witty and amusing glance at Manojan.

Manojan: I simply had a doubt, that's all.

Sumesh lets out a long hum.

Manojan raises the shovel and positions it horizontally, with one end on his shoulder and the other on Sumesh. A wide shot of the market crossroads as the scooter slowly moves away. The screen fades to black, and then the title appears.

A Nutty Affair

A drone shot starts from the lush green coconut groves surrounding a traditional, old ancestral home. The camera then slowly zooms in to reveal the house's intricate wooden architecture and traditional Kerala-style tiled roof. The shot ends with Manojan stepping out of the house and heading towards his vehicle parked outside.

Manojan resides someplace close to the Malabar region in an old ancestral home known as "Cheriyandi Plakkal."

Cheriyandi Plakkal was once located in the district of Kannur, but it is currently in the district of Kasargod. The Land of Seven Languages, also known as the Land of Kasaragod, is a region in Kerala, India's southernmost state. The name "Kasaragod" is derived from the Malayalam word for a fortified palace, reflecting the area's rich history of royal rule.

One of the unique features of this region is that it is home to seven different languages: Malayalam, Tulu, Kannada, Konkani, Marathi, Beary, and Urdu. This linguistic diversity has contributed to the area's rich cultural heritage and has resulted in a vibrant and colorful mix of traditions and customs.

The Land of Kasaragod is also known for its natural beauty, with stunning beaches, lush green hills, and an abundance of flora and fauna. It is this unique blend of culture and nature that makes the Land of Seven Languages so special.

Manojan was born on May 24, 1984, the same day Kasaragod was moved from Kannur, so the family and neighbourhood always remember that day.

May is the month of school vacation. Cousins of the same age group who have come to celebrate Manoj's birthday at their Cheriyandi Plakkal house

When Manojan arrived, wearing his birthday dress with pride, a cousin from Kannur approached him.

Manojan replied to a question from his cousin, and when he replied that the egg came first, everyone made fun of him and said that even a baby knows that the chicken came first.

Again on May 24, the moment they caught sight of his father, they jumped off the tree without alerting Manojan. Even though everyone else was plucking and throwing parangi (cashew) mangoes at each other that day, Manojan was punished by his father by being locked in a room at the Cheriyandi Plakkal for plucking the immature green cashew nuts.

Everyone used to celebrate May 24th this way, while Manojan decided that his birthday was not something to be celebrated.

One of the most frequent discussions his aunts have with his father to keep their kids away is that Manojan has some problem somewhere.

The screen dissolves from the flashback scene.

CHAPTER 4

KIDS' SHOW

Morning/Ext.

It was a pleasant morning. Besides the Cheriyandi Plakkal house to the left, there are ten cents of land on which an old pandal warehouse stands tall.

Manojan's father, Vijayan (65), is in the shamiyana pandal business. Outside that warehouse, Shamiyana items like red plastic chairs and large cooking vessels are neatly stacked, and two goods carrier vehicles (Ape) are parked. Vijayan walks towards the warehouse with a white sleeveless vest and designer lungi. A Bengali labourer named Babu is loading a large stack of chairs onto the parked carrier vehicle.

Vijayan asks Babu as he turns to face him.

Vijayan: Did Manojan come here?

Babu: Mujhe maaloom nahin…

Vijayan: What about Sumesh?

Babu: Mainne dekha nahin… Modalali (Master)

As he enters the warehouse, Vijayan gives him a quick glance.

Cut to

Manojan came there on his dusty scooter. While he parks the bike in the stand, he looks at Babu who is loading red plastic chairs onto the carrier, and asks him

Did father come here?

Manojan attempts to lift a heavy cloth bag from his scooter. Babu claims not to have seen him lift that and responds

Babu: Mujhe pata nahin….

As Manojan carries his bag inside the warehouse, continues his monologue

Whatever you ask him, his answer will always be the same "Dekha Nahni... Maaloom Nahin.. Pata Nahin…."

Manojan enters the warehouse with the bag and starts removing the small curry vessels, spatulas, and spoons from it, keeping them in a corner. Vijayan enters after hearing the noise.

Vijayan: Did you meet Purushan while coming?

Manojan: Yeah.. I met him. My cashew nuts are more yellowish he says

Vijayan: Not about that. Didn't he tell you about his son's birthday, why don't you do it for him?

Manojan turns around and walks away without showing any interest. While walking away he murmurs

He is a renowned miser and I am sure he will not pay us the agreed amount. Besides, And that too, the birthday of that dumb son of his… Furthermore, it's a kids' show, so what will we gain from that? He had requested you, right? Why don't you take it over?

Vijayan appears helpless as Manojan leaves. Manojan starts his scooter and rides away.

CHAPTER 5

THE ONE & ONLY EVENT MANAGER

Day/Ext.

The camera is mounted on the outside of the vehicle, shooting from the front, capturing Manojan's profile as he travels through the village.

The cool breeze seeps inside the small window of an ape vehicle heavily loaded with pandal goods while Manojan carefully drives through the narrow lanes of his village. Sumesh follows the vehicle on his scooter, while Babu is seated on top of it. They enter a house that has been neatly decorated for a wedding.

The vehicle is parked on the right side of the house. Seeing the vehicle with pandal goods, Groom's father Gangettan comes running towards and asks Manojan

Manoja, did you drive along the narrow lane with so many goods loaded? Don't you have a driver?

Manojan: No, but Sumesh is following us.

Gangetan: I thought you may not come as it is a very small event.

Manojan: After we do all the work, people don't pay us even the pandal rent. How will I pay both the labourer and the driver? That's why I manage alone.

Sumesh stops the bike and comes to Manojan. Manojan is looking at Sumesh.

Manojan: My father and this guy compelled me, Isn't it Sumesh?

Sumesh looks at Manojan and nods his head, indicating a yes. Gangettan goes behind the vehicle and instructs Bengali Babu

Bhaiyya.., ye sab idhar se udhar... ok...

Babu: Chetta, you also help me, anyways Chettan is not going to pay the full amount...right?

Gangettan gave Babu a questionable stare.

Purushan walks into Gangettan's house, leaving his bike parked to one side. He looks at Gangettan and queries

Gangettan..., arrangements are going on in full swing, isn't it?

Purushan notices Manojan seated inside the ape vehicle while speaking with Gangettan.

Purushan: Gangetta... just a minute...

Gangettan goes to Purushan.

Purushan: Didn't you get anyone else better than this LLB guy? There were so many talented event planners in our town, and they could have done an excellent job for much less money.

Manojan notices Purushan, who is turning away from him, and shrugs it off, turning the steering wheel and cleaning the speedometer with no regard for Purushan.

Gangettan: It's only because of my close relationship with Vijayettan I demanded to erect his Pandal and its nothing to do with this guy

Purushan: He thinks he's a big event manager, so he doesn't like all this.

Manojan gets out of the vehicle and sits on Sumesh's bike, puts on the helmet, starts the bike, and rides away. Close-up on Gangettan and Purushan's faces as they look towards Manojan riding away, giving a mocking smile.

CHAPTER 6

'LLB' WAS WASTED

Night/Int.

The camera is positioned inside the dimly lit dining room, with Sumithramma, Manojan's sixty-year-old mother, in the foreground setting the table and the moonlit night visible through the window in the background. The sound of crickets fills the room. Vijayan comes towards the table and pulls up a chair to have his dinner, looking around and asks

Did Manojan have food?

Sumitramma serving red boiled rice to Vijayan from a steel vessel

Sumitramma: You have your food; he will come only after having a bath

Vijayan sighs and starts to eat. Manojan comes to the table wearing a t-shirt after bathing, takes a plate, and serves himself rice and curry.

As he continues to eat, Vijayan turns to face Manojan and says

As you said, I went looking for a slightly bigger carrier vehicle and they said there is a new model arriving next week. When they call, you go and have a look. If you feel it's good, we shall exchange the old for the new one.

Manojan: There is no use changing the vehicle, only those who have an event management company need such vehicles. Additionally, I just got started with my cashew nut business.

In between glances at Manojan, Vijayan places some curry on his plate.

Vijayan: We are already into the pandal shamiana business right? Do we really need another business?

In response, Manojan gulps some water from the full glass and says

Manojan: That's what I said, we don't require such vehicles

Sumitramma comes to serve curry to Manojan but he stops her and says

Manojan: Enough, I wasted my time studying LLB to look after this pandal business, isn't it?

Manojan raises his head to stare at his mother's face.

Manojan: I told you before that I wasn't capable of studying LLB, Now, wherever I go to erect pandals, I get mocking glances from people.

Close-up on Manojan as he gets up and walks to the sink to wash his hands. Cut to a medium shot of Sumithramma looking at Vijayan's face.

CHAPTER 7

A Hard-Hit

Day/Ext.

The expanse of the municipal grounds and the two characters sitting in the foreground are captured in this wide shot from a low angle.

Manojan and Sumesh are relaxing on a windy evening on the municipal grounds. Children can be seen playing cricket in the distance. They are enthusiastically engaged in the game. A ball thrown by one of the children is heading straight for Manojan and Sumesh. Seeing the flying ball, Manojan panics. He immediately gets up and moves away. Sumesh picks up the ball and throws it back to the children. Manojan looks at it and says

Dude, I was frightened! How courageously do these young people bat? Do you recall our youthful days?

Subish, a buddy of Sumesh who is seated next to him, says at that point

Isn't that the tale of Sumesh's twisted ball? We will never forget that.

Manojan: The only thing I can recall is the ball bouncing in my direction.

Sumesh: That day in the hospital, Vijayettan questioned me, "Didn't he use a groin pad while batting?"

Subhish intervened.

Did you actually wear one that day, brother?

Manojan: Hey no! from that day onwards I only remember I have never stepped out on the ground to bat

A ball hit by another boy rolled near Manojan. He saw that and said

Enough already! Never call me to watch them play. Come on, please let's go. These kids can never be trusted!

medium shot from behind, showing Manojan and Sumesh walking out of the municipal grounds.

CHAPTER 8

Nutty Nuisances

Eve./Int./Ext.

A wide shot of the sky: the moon can be seen in the sky, and the sun is trying to soften the day. The weather is cold today. Manojan sitting on the veranda precisely seals the cashew nut packets which have a neat multi-colored label on them 'Manoj - Export Quality Cashew Nuts' with the tagline 'Eat Manoj's Cashew Nuts for Stronger Mental & Physical Health,'

On his phone, a video of a large cashew factory was playing, and the sound could be heard throughout the entire home. Manojan's mother Sumithramma comes out to Manojan and asks,

Manoja...Meethelechery's Devi's son's wedding is tomorrow right?, if our vehicle is going there, can you drop me there in the morning? I can't climb the hill because of this leg pain.

Manojan: Didn't someone tell you, they are all modernized nowadays? They have handed it over to an event management company, we and our business is all outdated now and the saddest part is that we haven't realized yet

Sumithramma: Your father told that you were busy tomorrow with an event already booked, I thought it would be the same wedding.

Manojan in a teasing manner refers to his father

Manojan: Umm... What booking? Maybe Poovadukkam Purushan's son's birthday party. I smelt this when he was showing excessive love towards father. Do you think he will pay us the pandal rent?

Sealing the cashews in plastic packets

Manojan: My dream is to have Manoj International Events & Exports function together in our 10-cent land.

Ashwathy, Manojan's elder sister, is mentioned by Sumithramma as she sighs.

Ashwathy had called me and I said I will come there directly.

Manojan: Ah! Then only both of you should go, I will not come. Those two wicked kids of hers will be there always running behind me shrinking "Mama, Mama". Utter 'Nuisance'!

Sumithramma: Nuisance? Don't say that.

Manojan: Just like their father, they have no respect for elders. Fools!

As she leaves, Sumithramma turns to face Manojan and says

I don't understand what happens to you when you hear the word children. Come inside. I'll serve you the food. Your father will be late I guess.

CHAPTER 9

An Extra Mile

Morning/Ext.

The camera pans across a serene and quiet suburban neighbourhood. The street lamps are still on, casting a warm glow over the area. A medium shot shows Vijayan stepping onto the footpath, wearing his walking shoes, and carrying a water bottle. The camera follows him with a tracking shot as he starts his morning walk.

A wide shot shows a few other pedestrians on the road. The camera then zooms in on Vijayan as he picks up pace and joins the flow of walkers.

A high-angle shot captures the entire scene, showing the peaceful neighbourhood waking up to a beautiful Sunday morning.

A midshot of William Lawyer walking towards Vijayan William Lawyer approaches Vijayan with a smile on his face. Close-up of Vijayan's face as he turns to face William and a two shot of William and Vijayan talking

Vijaya, I will walk the extra mile today.

Vijayan: So what lawyer Sir? I will also walk that extra mile with you

William Lawyer: I know that you will walk with me if I ask you for that.

Vijayan: Haha..Why not a lawyer Sir? After our lawyer says, there is no appeal against it.

The lawyer walks briskly, swinging his hands. Vijayan also walks beside him. After they walk a little further

Vijayan: Kuryachan told me that you have bought a new flat. He is the secretary of that flat, isn't he?

William Lawyer: Just for a change I bought it, not that it was essential. That's what he told you? Didn't he say anything else?

Vijayan: He told me that as soon as you shifted there, he lost his peace of mind. What issue did you raise there?

William Lawyer: Hmm... That guy Kuryachan is a crooked green-eyed serpent, that's why I smacked his head so that he doesn't think of biting me ever.

William lawyer stops near a closed petty shop and tells Vijayan

You know me right? I am one of those people who come home pretty late at night. Whenever I come, the flat gate remains closed. No matter how much ever I blow the horn, they won't open it. One day I scolded the security guy. I told him I shall file a case against him, and you should have seen his fearful reaction.

Vijayan: Oh..so that's the matter...

William Lawyer: Vijaya, I've brought a civil lawsuit against him, for denying someone entry to his own home.

The lawyer proudly looks at Vijayan's face and continues

I was already behind Kuryachan for a long time, right now he might be the secretary, yet we won't know his destiny until the court ruling is out.

Vijayan: I believe Kuryachan could only have instructed the security to trick you. You're doing the proper thing. Anyone else would have made the same decision as you did.

William Advocate grins as he looks at Vijayan. Vijayan opined

Lawyer Sir, the truth will win out.

Vijayan and William are seen walking down the road in a long shot.

CHAPTER 10

A Startup

Night/Ext.

A medium shot of Manojan and Sumesh sitting on the verandah, the verandah floor is quite a cool place at night for some chit-chat, with the exterior of the house visible in the background.

Sumesh: So, what do you mean? your father isn't interested in your event management startup

Manojan: No, That's not going to happen, I convinced him several times that I shall manage with the vacant 10 cents behind the warehouse, but…

Sumesh's wife Suja walks out to Manojan with a smile, says

Manojetta, don't leave without eating dinner.

Manojan: No need, Suja; all I was thinking was that I might leave a little later. They haven't gone to sleep yet; those kids are still playing there.

Suja: Is Ashwathiechi also here?

With a grumpy face looking at Suja, Manojan grumbles about Shinoj Kunjhikannan Ashwathi's husband who is with the Karnataka state police force for quite some time now

Manojan: Shinoj is now in the Karnataka Police, so I feel the job has been more of a leisurely affair for him

Sumesh: Manojaa... Isn't having kids around the house a positive thing?

In response, Manojan turns to face Suja and says

Now, I know you'll have a similar feeling.

Manojan gets up to leave, while Suja turns to Manojan

The last time when I met Ashwathi chechi, she was talking about your wedding.

Manojan: I think it's because she did not find anything to gossip about

Manojan picks up the torch that is kept close to the pillar and turns it on. He then walks out of Sumesh's house, which is in his neighborhood.

Manojan: Ok then, Good night

Sumesh and Suja watch Manojan with the torch as he gradually fades away in the darkness; and Suja mentions Maalu, Manojan's younger sister

Suja: Oh! I forgot to ask him when Maalu's delivery date was confirmed.

Sumesh: Hmm, the best person to ask, he doesn't know the name of his own sister's kids and you expect him to know his other sister's delivery date. Come, let's go inside, and serve me dinner. I'm feeling very tired today.

A close-up of Manojan's face as he walks away with the torch is followed by a medium shot of Sumesh and Suja on the verandah watching him.

The camera then moves to a long shot of the house and its surroundings as Manojan disappears into the darkness. The sound of crickets fills the silence as the scene fades to black.

CHAPTER 11

Hands Up

Night/Ext.

A close-up shot of the gate makes a quiet creak as it slowly opens, followed by a medium shot of Manojan walking towards the house in the dimly lit surroundings.

Ashwathy's son Prasoon aged 7 runs towards him with a black toy gun in his hand aiming at his head and Manojan moves aside

Maama... I will shoot you.

Manojan yells, shaken and terrified by the unexpected attack.

Manojan: Can you just keep that away, What if it bursts?

Prasoon refers to Prabhi his younger brother aged 5, who is also in the mood to play with his uncle screeching at him

Prabhi... Come fast!!! I have arrested uncle.

Prabhi also comes running, and they both surround him and force him to raise his hands.

'If you don't raise your hands, I'll shoot you, Uncle'

Manojan enters the house with both his hands raised, followed by the children. Ashwathy and Mother laugh at the situation Manojan is in. Shinoj, the father of the kids, comes in wiping his hands on his lungi after having his dinner.

Shinoj: Hah! Well done, my kids; at least you were able to lock him up; and saved the Karnataka state police department's reputation.

Manojan looks at Shinoj and tries to lower his hands. Looking at that, Prasoon signals Prabhi to surround him again yelling

Prasoon: Maama.. don't lower your hand. If you lower your hand I will shoot you.

Looking at that, Ashwathy sighs and says

They always ask me about Manoj Maman. They don't have any kids to play with in our staff quarters.

Shinoj: I don't mind if they stay here for a few days. It will be a happy time for both father and mother.

Children leave Manojan and rush into Vijayan's room, firing the toy gun.

Manojan: Nobody here has time for such a time to pass. Amma, serve me dinner.

The camera remains static as Manojan speaks and then pans slightly to the right to follow him as he walks to his room.

Dissolve and cut

The camera follows Vijayan, and Vijayan walks out of his room to the verandah. Children also follow Vijayan to the verandah, Ashwathy talks to Vijayan while trying to stop the children

Achcha, you should get him married as soon as possible. Did you see his guise, hair, and beard, I feel he is going to be a sanyasi. As Shinojettan says, how can we leave Prasoon and Prabi here, don't they have school?

If there is a house.., it should have children.., isn't it..?

Shinoj weighs between

Shinoj: Have you ever noticed how his face and behaviour change when he hears the names of our children? As if a cockroach were trapped in a glass bottle, People are saying that Aliyan (brother-in-law) is scared of children. Is it a kind of disease that I haven't ever heard of?

Right then, Shinoj is startled and runs inside when he hears a dog barking in the background, seeing this

Ashwathy: How about this? Each person is afraid of something different.

Shinoj: But I have heard about this one for the first time

Vijayan: I have tried a lot. Now you people can give it a try.

Shinoj: If he doesn't want a girl from this village, then we will try from Karnataka. Just like the way I got married to Ashwathy.

Putting on a stern expression, Ashwathy looks at Shinoj.

Still fearful of the dog, Shinoj keeps a suspicious eye on the outside. A close-up of Ashwathy and Sumithramma's faces as they giggle at each other.

CHAPTER 12

A RIPE PAPAYA!

Day/Ext.

The rear of Manojan's residence. The camera is positioned at a slightly elevated angle to capture the entire scene. Sumithramma is seated close to the pandal godown in the glaring daylight. She had come down to visit the godown just as Bengali Babu stacked the pandal materials on top of each other. Shobana Ettathi (Sister), Sumithramma's kitchen helper, comes with a broom in her hand.

Shobana Ettathi: Sumithra Ettathi... Maalu's delivery date isn't the 22nd of this month, is it?

Sumithramma: Yeah! The doctor said so. I just hope that it shouldn't be a cesarean as it happened in Aswathy's case.

Shobanettathi: Exactly Sumithraettathiye, Remember, you had told me about Manojan? There is a girl in our place. She has very beautiful, fair, long hair too.

Vijayan passes by them, heading towards the warehouse. Shobanettathi looks at him and mentions him.

Shobanettathi: I have seen a girl for Manojan. Cheemeni area folks. She isn't a well-educated Vijayetta, but a very nice girl. If he goes on telling everyone that he has an LLB then he might not get any proposals.

Vijayan: What do you mean? Didn't he have to put in extra effort to get that degree?

Shobanettathi: Vijayetta, everyone in our village knows that he didn't complete the course. If you keep aside her education, these folks are really nice people.

Vijayan looks at Sumithramma as she silently chops a lime-green papaya.

Vijayan: Let me ask him once.

Vijayan walks away briskly, and Sumithramma keeps looking at Vijayan. Shobana washes her hands before helping Sumithramma. She wants to know as she gathers papaya peels.

What if this Papaya rips?

Shobana draws Sumithramma's attention.

Sumithramma: Haven't you seen a Papaya ripe?

Shobanettathi: That girl is just like that, A ripe Papaya!

Shobanettathi's face is centered in the frame at a low angle.

CHAPTER 13

FREEDOM OF EXPRESSION!

Day/Ext.

Manojan and Sumesh are present on a beautiful day at the girl's house, and after a formal introduction, Manojan and the girl, Bindu, are standing in the shade of a wide cashew nut tree.

The camera is positioned at a low angle, looking up towards Manojan and Bindu, with the branches of the cashew nut tree framing them in the shot. Manojan, holding a branch of the tree, stands next to Bindu and asks her.

So you're not interested in a forcible marriage. That is also my opinion. Moreover, if it is for society and the family you get married to, then not at all interested. What about you Bindu...

Bindu: Me too

Manojan: Particularly, children after marriage. No one is worried about our country's population. Have you ever assumed what might happen to our country if the population keeps growing? What is your opinion?

Bindu: Children means life to me. And I've never thought about how having kids will impact the development of our country.

Bindu takes a quick look at Manojan's eyes and says

Bindu: If babies are born, then I wish that they were twins, that's what my opinion is.

Manojan's face is shown in close-up. Right then, a ripe cashew apple with the nut fell at his feet, and the camera quickly cuts to a low-angle shot of a ripe cashew apple falling at Manojan's feet, followed by a medium shot of Bindu laughing out loud.

The camera then switches back to a close-up of Manojan's face, which turns red with embarrassment, and he quickly looks down at the cashew apple, hoping to hide his face.

Dissolve to

Manojan is sitting in the car in which they had traveled to the girl's place. Bindu's uncle softly tells Sumesh as they move towards the car.

Uncle: Manojan might have his individual opinion about everything since he has studied LLB, right?

Sumesh nods and replies

Yes... Yes. Freedom of expression!

close-up on Uncle's face as he stares at Sumesh with surprise, while Sumesh walks towards the car in the background.

CHAPTER 14

Precious Golden Shawl

Day/Int.

On a lazy afternoon, Kunjipalan, the Panchayat president, and Prafulan, the local area secretary, enter the warehouse office and sit in the two chairs that are set up in front of Vijayan, who is carefully going over the large pending payments account book.

Over the shoulder shot of Vijayan as he flips through the pages of the account book, with Kunjipalan and Prafulan visible in the foreground, seated in chairs facing him.

Referring to the political party function to be hosted with Poorakkali dance, a folk art performed in the Malabar region of Kerala, Prafulan speaks up.

Prafulan: Mainly we have 'Poorakkali', just like every year we conduct

Kunjipalan: Since it is a matter of our party, we know that Vijeyettan will surely do his best, but regarding payment...

Prafulan interferes in between and continues

It is for the party, just like Kunjhiettan said, Vijayetta, we will honour you with a 'Ponnada' (Shawl)

Vijayan: There are a lot of Ponnadas lying here, Prafula, I hope you understand it's not possible to run my business with just 'Ponnada'.

Kunjipalan: Everything will happen in a good way Vijayetta. And we are always there for you.

Vijayan: Hell is going to break loose! only that's going to happen. Manojan is never interested in these party programs. Moreover, the school has organized its youth festival on the same day. Every year they order us to manage the event and the association pays in cash immediately after the celebration.

Prafulan: We are not here for Manojan. We are requesting you because of our closeness to Vijayanetta, we will be there for you always... isn't it President?

A close-up shot of Vijayan's face as he asks while nodding his head

Do you want to have tea?

Camera on Kunjhiettan and Prafulan's faces, showing their confusion and bewilderment.

CHAPTER 15

UNSTABLE MELODY

Day/Ext.

One moment, a long, dry dirt storm blew over the school's ground. A youth festival is being held on the school grounds, with the children neatly dressed in PT uniforms and parents and teachers wearing badges moving around the grounds and arranging things.

A bird's-eye view of the ground shows children running around and Manojan's ape goods vehicle slowly driving towards the pandal work area.

The final stabilizing and fixing of the pandal and the stage are in progress. Manojan physically checks the steps onto the stage. Sumesh is arranging the chairs, and Bengali Babu is standing on a ladder, tying a part of the pandal, while shyly giggling at the girls standing beside the stage.

Purushan, his pregnant wife, and their two children are sitting at the front of the stage. A medium shot shows Surabhi Teacher standing on the side of the stage, with children performing in the background. As the children approach her and talk about the program, the camera zooms in for a close-up shot of Surabhi's face, emphasizing her role as the program coordinator and her interaction with the children.

Cut to

Diljit, Purushan's fifth-grade son, performs on stage while singing a well-known Kannada melody. The camera focuses on his face as he pours his heart into the performance, and the audience can be seen swaying to the rhythm of the music. Manojan is also enjoying the song among the audience. After a few minutes, Manojan tells Sumesh that he is leaving.

Manojan notices Surabhi Teacher, The camera zooms in on Manojan and Surabhi as their eyes meet, then cuts to a shot of Manojan walking away, but the focus remains on Surabhi, who is still smiling.

Suddenly, Diljit, who was singing the song melodiously, is hit by one of the pandal rods as a major portion of the stage collapses. Manojan hears the sound of collapse and turns around; Purushan, Surabhi teacher, and a few other people can be seen rushing to the stage.

CHAPTER 16

Main Ne Kiya Nahin, Mujhe Maloom Nahin

Day/Int.

Inside the warehouse, Manojan's screams could be heard. Manojan, trying to pacify himself out of the situation, scolded Bengali Babu in a loud voice.

Didn't I tell you in Malayalam? No matter what, you only have one answer: 'Maaloom nahi, pata nahi'. Just say the same thing to the police when they enquire, Ok?

Babu: Police!!! Meine kuch kiya nahin ... mujhe pata nahi.

Manojan: Ah! But for the Police everything is maaloom.... Negligence of duty IPC section 330, 323/34, and 304(2) Indian penal code.

The camera focuses on Bengali Babu's face, showing his expression of confusion and fear.

Cut to

Babu is sitting on the ground outside the warehouse, a few meters away, rolling some paper to himself as a bullet bike comes to a halt in the yard. The camera shows a close-up shot of the bullet bike's front wheel as it comes to a halt, kicking up a small cloud of dust. Babu looks stunned at the man wearing a formal blue-colored checked shirt over Khakhi trousers and well-polished, shining brown shoes.

The camera then pans up to show the rider getting off the bike. Shinoj walks inside the warehouse without noticing Babu. Babu stays stoned even after Shinoj moves in and meets Manojan and strikes up a conversation

Shinoj: What is this Aliya? That's why I always say that this pandal business will only cause trouble. As you wish, even if you start an event management company or cashew nut company, this will be the plight.

Manojan: If you have come to see my father, he is at home

Shinoj: As soon as I heard about this, I started from my station. I will talk to Purushan in my style. He won't go to the police. If he does then you know me. I will file a POSCO case against him. 'Karnataka Police andre gottilla avanige... *'* (Talking in the Kannada language: He doesn't know the power of karnataka police.)

Bengali Babu sheepishly peeks inside the warehouse. Shinoj observes Babu and Babu is fretful

Shinoj: Aliya, it's better we wind up this pandal business, build a shopping complex and rent it out. It will be a source of income for Ashwathy and their children in the future. Ashwathy has no interest in this and doesn't know about all this, Okay?

During this conversation, Babu comes in and innocently stands in front of Manojan with a bundle of clothes.

Babu: Meine kiya nahin... mujhe maaloom nahin.

The camera focuses on Shinoj's face, as he appears confused and oblivious to what's happening with Babu. Manojan frustrated looks at Babu, and shouts at top of his voice in anger as if he intended to yell at Shinoj

Manojan: Take this and get lost man.

The camera cuts back to Manojan, who is still fuming with anger, as he storms off towards the warehouse.

CHAPTER 17

FAKE FRACTURE

Day/Int.

The camera is positioned high in the air. A tilt shot showing an aerial view of the school compound then cut to two shot.

Manojan is very tensely seated in front of the bespectacled headmaster in his chamber when the school bell rings. Manojan carefully listens to the headmaster

Headmaster: Two kids from 3B have sustained injuries. However we can ignore them as minor injuries, But Diljit's right leg got fractured. His father was threatening to go to the police station and file a report.

Manojan: Sir, I know Purushan very well. He is simply creating a ruckus by calling it a fracture. Nothing else

Surabhi comes to the Headmaster's chamber with a ledger book in her hand and waits near the door. The headmaster summons her to come inside. She comes in and opens the ledger book which has all the program bills in it and shows it to the headmaster

Surabhi: Sir, now only refreshments and Pandal bills are pending

Headmaster: You settle the refreshment bills

The principal murmurs while eyeing Manojan.

Headmaster: Let the pandal bills be pending

Manojan: Sir, the incident happened because of the negligence of my worker. There is no use holding up my payment. That Purushan is simply scaring you with the police case and all…

Manojan tells the headmaster as Surabhi looks up at him in a low, pleading manner.

Sir, it happened unexpectedly and there are witnesses and camera footage as evidence. There is no specific section for this incident, so a case cannot be filed.

Headmaster: Are you teaching me law? If possible go and pay at least half of the hospital bill of that child. Since it happened in the school, I will be held responsible for all this

Manojan: Yes Sir, I understand it is your responsibility. If you settle my full bill now, I will settle half of the hospital bill, how about that?

Headmaster seems restless and in a confused state to settle down the issue and says to Surabhi

Headmaster: Teacher, just settle his bill too

Surabhi nods and looks at Manojan. The headmaster indicates to her to leave she leaves the room with the ledger, while the camera slowly zooms in on Manojan's face as he speaks to the Headmaster

Manojan: Sir, anyway next year's youth festival should be celebrated as a mega event, what's your opinion?

CHAPTER 18

LAW POINT

Day/Ext..

Low-angle shot showing the grandeur of the town session court building with the bright blue sky and fluffy white clouds in the background. People in black coats are moving around while Purushan is talking to someone outside the session court gate. William lawyer lazily walking towards the court sees Purushan and asks him

William: Mr. Purushan, you wasted a wonderful opportunity

Purushan: What sort of an opportunity lawyer?

William: I know Vijayan personally, he is a good man. But that doesn't solve your problems, right?

Purushan: Oh...You were talking about that incident

William: I thought you would come to me. Such matters shouldn't be solved mutually. We should rightfully get what we deserve. Why are we here as lawyers then?

Purushan: Lawyere... Manojan started throwing law points at me. On top of it, the injury wasn't that serious either.

Purushan receives a cunning smile from William.

William: Now if you have decided everything, what can I say? So you too were subdued by Manojan's law point, isn't it?

Purushan: Diljit has started going to school now, Lawyere...

William: I thought you would at the least file a police case. Not just Manojan, I even know how to lock up his father Cheriyandi Plakkal Vijayan. Anyways, it's ok. I will leave.

medium shot of William walking away.

CHAPTER 19

Kannada Teacher

Day/Ext.

Medium shot, showing Manojan and Sumesh standing or sitting near the Thejaswini River's bank, with the river visible in the background.

Sumesh: Surabhi teacher called Suja and said that the children have started coming to school.

Manojan: Don't remind me of that incident... I have decided I shall never use my law points with anyone. But what to do? Sometimes people make me use that, and if I don't they won't let us live in peace.

Along the bank of the river, two people are rowing a boat at a distance. Sumesh watches them and says

Sumesh: Do you know the Kannada teacher at that school? She has enquired about you with Suja

Manojan: Was she Suja's classmate?

Sumesh: Suja told me she had even enquired about you several times

Manojan: I think they have nothing else to gossip about. I hope there are not many children in the Kannada class, incidentally which gives them more time for gossip

Sumesh smiling at this instant jest says

Sumesh: It's not that Manoja, I understand there's something fishy going on.

The camera focuses on Manojan's face as his expression changes, then fades to black, signaling the end of the scene.

CHAPTER 20

A Love Story

Day/Ext.

Montages

A bike can be seen in a broad valley covered in dry grass. Manojan rode his bike through the dry, grass-filled mountains. Relishing the solitude and silence of the open road. The music commences with a husky-toned male singer lending his voice to the lyrics

"You will feel the time of love in your heart

We can say it's a charming love to describe it

He finds a love like hers

You will feel the time of love in your heart...."

A close-up shot of Manojan's face as he takes in the beauty of the surroundings while riding the bike. The sun beat down on his back, casting a warm glow over the parched landscape. The hills around him, their slopes covered in golden grass that swayed in the breeze, a high-angle shot of the bike as it crests the hill, showing the expansive view of the valley below. Now he rides his bike through a lane; Surabhi is walking along the same lane; the bike is behind her; Surabhi moves to the side of the road upon hearing the sound of the bike. Manojan goes ahead on the bike without paying attention to Surabhi. Surabhi teacher looks at Manojan.

Montage

Poorakali season has begun in the village, and the song of Poorakali can be heard from afar. Surabhi and Manojan met at a Poorakkali place, a traditional dance form of North Kerala.

The air was filled with the sound of drums and cymbals as dancers moved in synchronized steps, their colorful costumes adding to the vibrant atmosphere. Surabhi and Manojan were drawn to each other, their eyes meeting across the crowded space.

"Singing songs that bring us joy,

We see the stars falling from the sky.

A sacred place, a place of love,

Light comes to us in time,

Filled with love, we become stars"

Montage

Manojan met Surabhi by the banks of the Chandragiri Puzha. A wide shot shows the river flowing peacefully. They were both mesmerized by the serene beauty of the river. Mid-shot of Manojan and Surabhi standing side by side, gazing at the river. As they sat by the river where Mani Ratnam shot his romantic film, Bombay, Surabhi mentioned how much she admired the character of Shaila Bano, played by Manisha Koirala, in Bombay. Manojan, who had not seen the film before, was intrigued and decided to watch it himself. The river became a symbol of their budding relationship. Amid Kerala's beautiful nature and mysticism A lovely affair is just beginning.

CHAPTER 21

A To-Do-List

Day/Ext.

Close-up camera angle on Surabhi and Manojan at a coffee shop. There's a fresh scent in the air, which fills up the new coffee shop in town. Surabhi and Manojans eyes lock up for a second and Manojan steadily distracts her with his talks

Manojan: There are a lot of things on my To-do-list

Surabhi: That's ok, if you are busy we will meet next Saturday

Manojan: No, I didn't mean that. I meant that there are many things unsettled in life. Surabhi must assure me that this wedding will not be a hindrance to achieving anything more in life.

Surabhi: What do you mean?

Manojan: Nothing..., Surabhi knows right, the next question after the wedding. And I don't believe in these societal routines.

Surabhi: Societal Routine. Is it about having children?

Manojan: Ha.. yes exactly. What is your opinion about children?

Surabhi: At present, I am spending most of the time in my life with the children, right? Hence, I have a good opinion.

Manojan: I heard someone saying that in America, they decide in advance not to have children after marriage and then they go ahead. Here in our country, they just get married to have children.

Surabhi looks at Manojan smilingly and says

Surabhi: Childless marriage, I don't know if that culture shall persist in our country. Right now I don't want to have children as I have just joined the school.

Manojan: That's right when there are children at school, there's no need for children at home. isn't it Surabhi?

A close-up shot of Manojan and Surabhi smiling at each other across a table, framed by the steam rising from their cups of coffee.

CHAPTER 22

Wedding Bells

Day/Int.

On a lengthy wooden table and bench laid horizontally along the wall inside the dimly lit staff room at one end of the school building, biology teacher Susamma and Raji Teacher are having lunch at the last corner table and speaking to themselves. A wide shot from a high angle, capturing the entire staff room with a focus on the last corner table.

Susamma Teacher: I heard, after that incident at school, everything started.

Raji Teacher: I heard that he is peculiar. I don't know what Surabhi liked in him. She could have got much better proposals, right?

Susamma: Moreover, they say he has also started a Cashew nut export business.

Raji Teacher: Do we really need to call that a cashew nut?

Raji teacher smiles and looks around and slowly mutters

Raji Teacher: It's better fun, in the local dialect of our village 'Andi (nut) business event,'

As they continue to chuckle, Surabhi teacher walks to the staff room and makes her comfortable at the first empty table in the row trying to open her lunch box while Susamma teacher towards Surabhi

Susamma Teacher: We were just talking about you, teacher

Raji Teacher: Is the date fixed, teacher?

Surabhi: No, may be in between the training

Susamma Teacher: No matter what, the teacher's wedding costs will be drastically reduced. I hope pandals and food will not be that costly.

Raji Teacher: In that case, Surabhi teacher is lucky

Smiling at the teachers, Surabhi opens the lid of her lunch box and starts to eat.

CHAPTER 23

MAMAN! ONCE AGAIN

Day/Int.

The place where a local tug-of-war competition is being held looks colorful and bright because of the colorful buntings and paper hoardings. As the participants pull the rope back and forth, the camera shows a view of them from a lower angle, with the colorful decorations in the background. This contrast highlights the intensity of the game and the festive atmosphere of the event.

As usual at any event, Babu is lazily unloading pandal goods from the Ape vehicle, and Sumesh is busy preparing the stage for the competition.

Manojan rides his bike steadily there. Seeing Manojan, Sumesh stops his work and comes to him, hurriedly looking at his mobile.

Sumesh: Vijayettan called me; he said he couldn't connect to your phone.

Manojan stops the bike and looks at Sumesh confused

Sumesh: Manoja, Maalu has delivered a baby, he has asked me to bring you along to the hospital. He says the baby is in the ICU.

Manojan: Let's finish the work first and then leave.

Manojan gets off the bike and pulls out some important things from the back of the bike and walks, while Sumesh to Manojan

Sumesh: You put that all down here and I will take care of it.

Manojan with no interest in what Sumesh is worried about, casually replies

Manojan: Then you also come with me...

Sumesh: Why are you tensed up? You became Maman once again, Manoj Maman!

Manojan starts the bike, while climbing on the bike Sumesh to Manojan

Sumesh: Hurry up! Be more active hereafter Mama.

The camera pans out to a wide shot from behind, showing the bike moving away from the camera.

CHAPTER 24

BABY BONKERS

Day/Int./Ext.

The shot begins with a wide-angle of the hospital building, showing the entrance with its glass doors. As the camera moves closer, we see Manojan standing near the glass room door, gazing into the hospital lobby. The camera then switches to a medium shot from behind Manojan, showing the busy hospital lobby and the nurses and doctors moving around attending to their patients. The shot ends with a close-up shot of the neonatal-NICU board. Vijayan and Sumithramma, both slightly panicked, are next to him. Manojan stands numb with no facial expression.

A wide glass ICU chamber where newborn babies are placed in rows was a sight of love and tenderness, while some babies could be heard crying from outside the glass room. Maalu's husband, Girish, walks in hurriedly with medicines in hand and hands them over to the nurse who just came out of the ICU.

Manojan: Is Maalu doing well?

Sumithramma: She is in the labour room. There's nothing to worry about.

Manojan gets uncomfortable in the ICU looking at the babies. One boy was screaming uncontrollably when his mother and the kid were sitting on a bench on the verandah. Manojan looks at everyone and tells Sumesh.

Manojan: Let's stand outside, I can't hear anything because of those babies crying.

Vijayan and brother-in-law Girish watch Manojan going out while Sumithramma asks Manojan.

Sumithramma: Have a look at the new born baby and leave

Manojan: I don't think I can stand and watch all this. You all are here, right? That's my only relief.

An uncomfortable Manojan hurriedly walks out. The camera lingers for a moment on the empty space where Manojan stood, emphasizing his absence and the uncertainty left in his wake.

CHAPTER 25

No Reply...

Day/Int.

As Surabhi enters the semi-special hospital ward, the camera is a medium shot from a low angle, emphasizing her presence and giving her an air of importance. The camera then switches to a close-up shot of Sumithramma's face as she looks up and sees Surabhi, her expression changing to one of happiness and relief.

The camera then pans out to a wide shot, showing the ward, with Maalu lying on the bed, Ashwathy placing the flask on the tabletop, and Surabhi's arrival creating a sense of hope and comfort in the room, looking at Surabhi Sumithramma happily.

Oh ! Surabhi... Suja had told me, when I called her, that you would come. Did you meet Manojan?

Surabhi: When I was about to arrive, I called him.. He didn't pick up the phone. No reply, He might be busy at work.

Ashwathy smiles at Surabhi, Surabhi sits next to Maalu

Surabhi: Don't worry, Suja said there is nothing to worry about.

Ashwathy: It's good that you came; I just told mom that I haven't met you in person.

Surabhi smiles at Aswathy and asks her

Surabhi: Where are the children?

Ashwathy: If they come, it will be difficult. Moreover, if they come, Manojan will not come, that's why I didn't bring them.

Surabhi smiles with a pause.

CHAPTER 26

REMEMBER 'SOCIAL ROUTINE'

Night/Int.

In a dimly lit, warm room, Surabhi is talking on the phone with Manojan. The lighting mood is warm and cozy, with soft lighting from a table lamp and dim overhead lights, creating a comfortable and relaxed atmosphere. A medium shot of Surabhi, with the camera slightly tilted to the side to give a sense of intimacy and closeness.

Manojan: That's why I decided, let's get married but kids....

Surabhi: Manojetta, whenever and whatever you speak, ultimately you end up with one subject 'children'

Manojan: Even if I tell you, you won't understand. Now I am thinking about whether I should get married or not.

Surabhi: What are you trying to say? I can't understand anything.

Manojan: Nothing, I just doubt whether this wedding is necessary.

Surabhi: What are you saying, didn't we decide everything beforehand?

Manojan: Surabhi, you remember everything we spoke about, right? Social Routine!

Surabhi: Childless...isn't it?

Manojan: Ho… That's enough, I am relieved.

Surabhi's mother enters Surabhi's room. Realizing that Surabhi is talking to Manojan, her mother says

Mother: Is it Manojan? Ask him whether Maalu and her baby are fine.

Surabhi covers up her phone speaker and tells her mother that she will ask later with a hand sign, and her mother walks out of the room smiling. The scene ends with the camera panning out further, showing the entire room and the comforting atmosphere it provides.

CHAPTER 27

THE 'GATTIMELAM'

Night/Int./Ext.

A retro Malayalam song is playing on huge speakers, and the whole family is excited and getting ready to celebrate Manojan's marriage, which was going to shortly happen in a nearby temple.

Wide Shot: Shows the entire family getting ready for the wedding, with the song playing in the background. *Close-Up Shot:* Zooms in on the speakers playing the malayalam song from the movie 'Meesa Madhavan' "Chingamaasam vannu chernaal nine njanen swanthamaakum" *Over-the-Shoulder Shot:* Shows a family member looking at Manojan as he gets ready. *Low-Angle Shot:* Camera placed at a low angle, making the family appear dominant. *High-Angle Shot:* Camera placed above the family, making them appear special. *Tracking Shot:* Follows Manojan as he walks towards the temple. *Bird's Eye View Shot:* Camera positioned high above the temple, showing the wedding ceremony. *Point-of-View Shot:* Shows the wedding ceremony from Manojan's perspective.

The whole of "Cheriyandi Plakkal's" house is decorated with flickering disco lights. The yard behind the kitchen is occupied with Manojan's neighbours, helpers, and the youngsters busy chopping vegetables on a steel table and arranging the chairs and the outside kitchen while Babu, with a big copper vessel inverted over his head, walks up and down the yard pretending to be busy.

At the temple, Ashwathy and Shinoj are with their kids, and Girish is standing near Maalu, who is carrying her newborn. Sumesh and his wife Suja, William Advocate and Vijayan, members of the Morning Walking and Clapping Club, and many more from their community neighborhood are all present there.

All the near and dear ones have surrounded the couple, especially Vijayan and Sumithramma, feeling happy and contented and blessing them while the "gattimelam" in the temple fills the air, giving it a holy wedlock ambience. Finally, Manojan, a married man, poses for the camera after tying the mangalsutra knots around Surabhi's neck.

The sight of Manojan's house with lights and buntings at the entrance has a very bright, festive vibe as children are playfully running around. There's a pleasant, warm feeling inside the house as the storm of celebration settles down at dawn.

Dissolve to

The children are playing on the bed with Surabhi. Manojan comes into the room, annoyed at the kids playing around, and speaks to himself.

All the gifts will be spoiled by these kids.

Manojan takes away all the gift boxes and neatly stacks them away on the table while Maalu's child is playing on the bed. Ashwathy enters the room as the children try to hide from her playfully. Manojan looks tensed and squeezes his face, saying

Manojan: These kids exactly carry the same character as their father. As in seeing robbers.

At the same time, Maalu enters the bedroom and bends down to carry her child to her other room, while Surabhi carefully lifts up the baby, kisses it on the forehead, and then smoothly hands the baby to Maalu.

Manojan is still busy stacking extra gift boxes lying on the floor on top of the cupboard in between the cashew nut packets without paying any attention to what's happening around him. Meanwhile, Ashwathy, trying not to disturb the newlyweds, summons her kids in a strict tone.

Ashwathy: Come here children, we are going to bed now. come out.

A medium shot of Ashwathy standing in the hallway, with the children walking past her towards their bedrooms.

CHAPTER 28

BRIGHT BALLOONS

Day/Int.

A pleasant summer day with everyone at home Children enjoy causing mischief and are constantly looking for new games to play, such as blowing up coloured balloons.

A close-up shot of the children's hands as they blow up the coloured balloons, showcasing the specific action and adding a bit of visual interest to the scene.

Prasoon: My yellow balloon is the biggest

Prabhi: Not at all. My pink colour will grow big

Prasoon: Do you want to see my yellow colour swelling bigger?

Prabhi: Then let's see. The yellow colour shall burst soon. You just wait.

Manojan comes home and walks into his room as usual, ignoring the kids. He looks around the room, which is filled with colored balloons lying on the floor. Manojan, in suspicion, immediately opens the door of his cupboard and hides behind it to watch Prasoon and Prabhi blowing up the balloons and playing with themselves. Shinoj comes out of the kitchen and notices Manojan looking suspiciously at the children. Prabhi runs towards Shinoj, hands him a packet of balloons, and screams.

Prabhi: Achcha, blow this up....

Shinoj looks at the colored packet in his hand with eyes wide open. Manojan looks at the condom in Shinoj's hand and they exchange an exclamatory look with each other

Prabhi: Prasoon, you just watch how big the pink balloon grows. Achcha! Stop looking at it like that and blow it up...

Prasoon's yellow balloon bursts with a boom. Prabhi claps and laughs, looking at the balloon burst. Manojan feels embarrassed.

Fade out and fade into a new scene with a caption reading

"Six lovely years have passed"

North Kerala experiences seasonal fluctuations. As the Tejaswini River flowed steadily, the sound of an old Malayalam song echoed through the air. Chekutty Chetan's shop radio at Market Junction was playing an old Malayalam song. "Unni va va vo, Ponnunni va va vo, Neela Peeli Kannum Pootti Pooncheladalo... Pooncheladalo" (A lullaby song)

Two recently built bridges spanned the river in the distance, connecting the two sides of town. Purushan now has a daughter too, Diljit's younger sister. Sumesh is also a parent, and Bengali Babu is still at Cheriyandi Plakkal House.

Bindu, once resembling ripe papaya, now resembles a good, sweet jackfruit, according to Shobetti. She also became a mother.

In the village's theaters, new films are constantly coming out.

Malayalam movies saw the debut of several new actors and actresses. Still, Mammootty and Mohanlal continued to be household names.

Kunjettan, the local Panchayat president, is running for MLA, and the local committee president, Prafullan, is now the Panchayat president of the village.

Gangettan now has a grandchild. All of the couples who married at Vijayetan's shamiyana pandal had children. All of Vijayetan's friends from the laughing club have become grandfathers. Kuriachan was being tricked by William Advocate using even more cunning tactics.

Every event was observed by the Cheriyandi Plakkal House, which stood tall.

CHAPTER 29

A Secret

Day/Int.

Morning or noon, lunch or recess, busy class or class off, there was sufficient time for all teachers in the staff room to engage in some gossip and chitchat. Susamma, a biology teacher, is talking to Raji in the staffroom during the morning recess.

Susamma teacher: It was a good decision made by Surabhi teacher not to have children till she completes her B. Ed, isn't it, Raji teacher?

Raji teacher smiles at her and replies

Raji teacher: Of course... Surabhi's teacher seems to have no time for some action I guess? If we ask her, she will show the children in her class and say that these are my children.

Susamma Teacher: No matter what? it isn't satisfying like having our own children, what do you say teacher?

Manojan comes near the staff room with a neatly packed, sparkling stainless steel lunch box in his hand, and the teachers immediately stop murmuring as soon as they see him. Manojan waits near the door of the staff room looking at the lengthy corridor while Raji teacher speaks to Manojan

Raji Teacher: Surabhi teacher might be still there in her classroom

Manojan: No problem, can you just give this to her

Raji Teacher: Why not? sure

Raji teacher receives the lunch box from Manojan, looking at that lunch box, Susamma Teacher smiles and softly responds

Susamma Teacher: Normally, it's children who forget these things

Manojan: There is no connection or theory attached to a child or adult who forgets small things. You may know that better being a biology teacher yourself and if by any chance there's new research done over this, kindly let me know, ok teacher.

Susamma goes mum upon hearing Manojan's reply. He leaves after giving back her words. Susamma lowers her voice and secretly looks up at what the Raji teacher tells her.

Susamma: Didn't I tell you, teacher, that he is of a peculiar type? Do you know, What Purushan told my husband about this guy?

Susamma teacher goes near Raji teacher and into her ear like disclosing the biggest secret of Manojan

Susamma teacher: He doesn't drink, he doesn't smoke, and God knows what all he doesn't do,

Both of them laugh. After a while, Susamma teacher picks up the textbooks on her table and prepares to go to her class while Raji smiles at her and confirms

Raji Teacher: Susamma teacher, don't share this secret with anyone else.

Susamma Teacher: Who? Me? Not at all...

A close-up shot of Raji Teacher's face as she watches Susamma Teacher leave the staff room. The camera then cuts to a medium shot of Susamma walking away from Raji, with Raji's gaze lingering on her. The camera then fades to black.

CHAPTER 30

Start Up & Down

Day/Int./Ext.

The camera is positioned at Sumesh's house, capturing his three and a half-year-old son Sonu as he playfully runs around the cool-covered veranda on a sunny day. Sonu trips and falls after tripping over a small plastic toy on the floor. Sumesh dashes over to him and picks up the child.

Suja: Now he keeps running all over the place. He runs and hides somewhere all the time.

Sumesh looks at Sonu and says

Sumesh: Is it, Sonu? Don't run away anywhere, ok?

Suja: I met Surabhi today and asked how about enrolling Sonu in the nursery.

Sumesh: Day by day, the daily expenses are rocketing. Events and orders are also less nowadays for Vijayettan, on the other hand, Manojan is still behind the startup plan of the event management company.

Suja: It's been so long he is behind this event management company start up plan, but nothing materialized ever, I think it's better for Sumeshettan to look for some better job.

Sumesh: Yeah, I know, At least Manojan can survive on the teacher's salary and his Cashew nut business.

The camera stays fixed on the veranda as Sonu, still playfully running around, puts the soft toy in his mouth. Suja, Sonu's caregiver, can be seen softly patting his tender hand and asking him to throw the toy away. The scene ends with Sonu looking mischievously at Suja before throwing the toy and running off.

CHAPTER 31

Grandparent's Wish

Night/Int.

The days seem to be humid, and the nights are cooler as Vijayan is near his bed getting ready to sleep. He is seriously thinking about something and arranging his bed as Sumithramma walks in with a matter ready at her lips.

Vijayan: You ask her once clearly, how do you think I can speak to him about this?

Sumithramma: Do you think it's something to be told and get done? They might have planned something.

Vijayan: Isn't Surabhi done with her training period yet? Then why the delay? The only relief is when Maalu and Aswathy visit us with their children. Sumesh also has a child, so I asked Sumesh too if Manojan had shared anything about it.

Sumithramma: Why do you have to roam around telling villagers about this?

Vijayan: It's not about Sumithra, didn't you get pregnant just three months after our wedding?

Sumithramma: So, I don't doubt that he can't prove the same. Moreover, what can we do except keep waiting for a grandchild? You go to bed, they have already gone to bed.

As Sumithramma finishes her dialogue, the camera slowly zooms out, revealing the quiet and peaceful surroundings of their house at night.

CHAPTER 32

FEAR OF CHILDREN

Day/Ext.

The camera slowly pans towards the bright daylight under the bus stop canopy, revealing Sukumaran, a smartly dressed medical representative, sitting on the bench. As the camera zooms in on his face, Sukumaran can be seen flipping through some pictures on his mobile while occasionally glancing up at the road. He sees Manojan in a medical shop across from where he is seated. Sumesh rides his bike there, stopping near where Sukumaran instructs him.

Sumesh: I haven't told him anything.

Sukumaran: That's fine. Anyways, we had decided not to tell him about this, then how shall we convince him? When I enter the doctor's room, I will give you a missed call and you can bring him over immediately. Ok?

Sumesh: Suku, isn't that better if we talk to the doctor about his specific problem?

Sukumaran: I know, but I have already explained that to the Doctor. You just bring him on time and Dr. Shanawaz will do the rest.

Manojan makes a quick stop as he approaches the two while talking to himself.

Sukumaran: F E A R O F C H I L D R E N !...

Suddenly Sukumaran looks at Manojan and cleverly changes the topic, turning towards Sumesh.

...yes..yes.. You should be fearing the children more than the adults, isn't it Sumesh?

Sukumaran looks at Manojan trying to reply to him, nodding his head continues

Sukumaran: It's not just that, but we should also try the possible methods from our end not to have children.

Manojan looks at Sukumaran weirdly and murmurs

Manojan: Are medical reps still there in town? Does their strategy still work to make doctors prescribe unwanted medicines?

Sukumaran throws Manojan a goofy but intelligent look as he responds.

Sukumaran: Umm! Sometimes, we must develop some strategies that consider patients.

Sukumaran looks at Sumesh with a smile while Manojan starts the bike and tells Sumesh

Manojan: These are the ones who really require treatment.

As Manojan finishes his dialogue, the camera focuses on Sukumaran's face, capturing his amused expression as he looks over at Sumesh. Now the camera angle is close to Sukumaran's face, magnifying his expression and emphasising the humour in the scene.

CHAPTER 33

JUST TEN CENTS

Day/Ext/Int.

Extreme Wide angle camera shot captures the vast expanse of the dry grassy terrain of north Kerala under a dreary blue sky filled with clouds. A black coloured Bullet bike is seen riding towards the west, creating a trail of dust behind it.

Shinoj's bike enters the main gate kept open and comes to a brief halt at Cheriyandi Plakkal's house. Shinoj in his police uniform and Aswathy seated behind him seem to be in a hurry as Ashwathy gets down quickly even before Shinoj parks the bike completely. Sumithramma and Vijayan come out as the bike enters.

Ashwathy: Where is he, Manojan? He is acting too smart...

Shinoj: Achcha, you know it right? Matter of that 10 cents land?

Ashwathy: He has told a broker to get it sold

Vijayan: Which one, our 10 cents?

Ashwathy: Other than that, what property do we have Achcha? You had told me long before that 10 cents is for me and my children, you remember? Moreover, he is already allergic to my children.

Sumithramma: Why are you so worried? Nothing has happened till now.

Vijayan: Yeah! First, you come inside, sit down, relax, I will tell you.

Vijayan sits, while Ashwathy and Shinoj walk inside.

Vijayan: I spoke to him about it. You know that he used to ask that land to start an event management company or that cashew nut company. When he insisted again and again, I told him that it is an ancestral property passed over by generations. I told him clearly since you don't have any children I cannot pass it over to you.

Sumithramma: Oh very good! And you never told me about this?

Vijayan: Didn't you tell me earlier, that it is of no use telling me what I need to tell him?

Vijayan looks at Shinoj and Ashwathy standing, walks up to them, and says

Vijayan: I am not going to give that property to anyone, and I don't want anyone to come here asking for it. I know what to do.

Vijayan walks inside while Shinoj fiercely looks at him and tells Ashwathy

Shinoj: I feel it is your father's idea, cunning fellow. You get me some water, I have a severe headache.

Cut to

After a while, Manojan enters the main gate, walks towards the verandah, and ignores all the people sitting there while Sumithramma stops him.

Sumithramma: Stop right here, what are you up to?

He stares at everyone sitting there and finally looks down at Shinoj and says

Manojan: That's what I even wanted to ask you? Amme, what are you all up to? Why did Aliyan speak to Purushan regarding the land?

Shinoj feels a little uncomfortable as Vijayan stares at him in disbelief.

Manojan: If you are planning to give me the land only after I have children, then that's not going to happen. And I'm making every effort on my end to avoid having children.

Ashwathy looks at Sumithramma in astonishment

Ashwathy: Amme, See, I told you, he has some problem

Manojan: Yes, I do have a problem, but how did it happen?... I have no intention of raising children by scaring, beating, and threatening them.

Ashwathy: Amme... Did you hear him? Seems like he too was abused.

The camera focuses on a two-shot of Manojan and Ashwathy talking, with a focus on Manojan's face. As he speaks, his face is a mix of rage, frustration, and sadness. The camera zooms in on Manojan's face as Ashwathy speaks, capturing the pain and hurt in his eyes.

CHAPTER 34

PLAN A KID

Day/Int.

On a bright Sunday afternoon, Surabhi is busy in the kitchen slicing bananas for the traditional Malabar snack known as unnakkaya. A close-up camera angle captures Surabhi's nimble fingers cutting the ripe bananas into small pieces as she hums a tune. The sound of the knife hitting the chopping board fills the air. Sumithramma enters the kitchen with a sorrowful expression on her face.

Sumithramma: Mole, consider me your Mother and don't feel bad about what I say

Surabhi: Never Amma, please tell me

Sumithramma: Now you have become a permanent employee in your school, I hope you both had decided not to have children till then, isn't it?

Surabhi: Yes Amma

Sumithramma: Vacation is about to start now and Mole, children are necessary for a house.

Surabhi: In the beginning, immediately after marriage, I insisted on Manojettan not thinking about having children. But as time passed by, Manojettan got angry even if I mentioned children.

Sumithramma: Even I have noticed that he has never touched Maalu's child. He keeps on giving excuses like he doesn't know how to hold a child and so on.

Surabhi: I shouldn't be saying this to you, but since you asked me I want to tell you, He doesn't even know Suja & Sumesh's son's name.

As Manojan's bike approaches their gate, Surabhi and Sumithramma abruptly end their talk. The camera captures their worried expressions as they look towards the door.

CHAPTER 35

A MASTER PLAN

Day/Ext./Int.

On a summer morning, the camera pans across the serene landscape away from the bustle of the town until it settles on Vijayan standing in front of an old building. He notices William Lawyer's office on the first floor of the building. Vijayan climbs the narrow wooden stairs to the office. On the first floor, as Vijayan is searching for William's lawyer's office, he sees Purushan coming out from one of the offices.

Purushan: Vijayetta, How come you are here?

Vijayan: Which one is the William lawyer's office?

Purushan: You see that second room in the verandah, that's his office; you can find his name board there

Vijayan finds the signboard, which reads "Advocate William Vincent," and walks inside the room. A husband and wife come out from the lawyer's cabin. Vijayan slowly opens the door and enters the cabin and William lawyer surprisingly asks Vijayan

William lawyer: Ho, Vijaya! Have you come to see me? I haven't seen you for a few days..? I hope you are on a casual visit here, sit down.

Vijayan: I have come to...

As he hesitates, William says, while glancing at Vijayan.

William Advocate: Tell me, Vijaya, I have to go to the court in a while

Vijayan: Lawyere.. Can we file a case for not having children?

The lawyer looked startled at Vijayan before coming close to his face and laughing suspiciously at him.

William Advocate: You did not impregnate someone at this age, did you? You brat?

Vijayan: It's not like that, I am just asking if there are no children. It has been 6 years since Manojan got married, but they still don't have a child.

William Advocate: You should be going to a doctor then, Go see a good gynecologist, and your job will be done. Vijaya, why did you come to a lawyer for this?

Vijayan: I guess you are busy, I will come later.

William Advocate: Hey... No hurry. This is the way we lawyers speak, ignore it. You tell me.

Vijayan: Lawyer… When we grow old, we wish for our grandchildren to be playing at home, don't you think so?

William Advocate: Of course! We will think, yes, we will.

Vijayan: We are tired by all means of asking Manojan and Surabhi. But Manojan gets angry at the words of a child. We want to see our grandchildren. Can't you find some way for us? That's the reason I came to you in the morning itself Lawyere.

William Advocate deeply thinks, rotating his pen with his eyebrow curved up leans back on his cozy black revolving chair muttering

William Advocate: Hmm! Mental harassment, mentally tortured by son and his wife. Isn't it? Anyways, that's enough, the case will hold good.

Vijayan: Lawyer, There is no such torture as you assume.

William lawyer: You feel so because you are so sober. Today's children, I tell you, if you just bow down, they shall pluck out and run away and that's how it is?

Wilson, aged 38 and the son of William the lawyer, dressed in a lawyer's coat, opens the door of William's cabin, walks in, and grabs the car keys hanging on the wall.

Wilson: Appa, I am taking your car. You don't have any urgency, right?

William lawyer: I have to go to the court

Wilson: Scooter is there.

Wilson takes the car key and leaves in a hurry. Vijayan turns to glance back at Wilson before turning his head to look at William lawyer, who tells him in a close-up camera shot.

William lawyer: Didn't you see that the present generation shall pluck out smartly if you bow? You go now leaving all worries, I'll take care of that, just come down when I call you. Be brave.

CHAPTER 36

A STRONG REASON

Night/Int.

A close-up shot of the kitchen sink, with the sound of running water filling the room. Ashwathy's hand is seen scrubbing a vessel vigorously. As she finishes cleaning the last utensil, she switches off the light, casting the room into darkness. The camera then follows her as she walks towards the bedroom, passing through the dimly lit hallway.

Shinoj at one end of the bed is reading a Malayalam magazine while Ashwathy unties her hair and comes near Shinoj to cuddle together for a few minutes before going to sleep when Shinoj asks her.

Shinoj: Did you fill the jug with water?

Ashwathy: No, anyhow, it is of no use. You can fill it up.

Shinoj goes and fills up the jug with water and places it on the side table.

Shinoj: Purushan, had come to the station today. He told me that he saw your father at Lawyer's office, But why did he go there?

Ashwathy: Why are you so tense? It might be a casual visit.

Shinoj: Your father is not the kind of person to visit a lawyer without a reason. There should be something important, that's my concern.

Ashwathy: Ah! He must have gone there to file a case against you...

Shinoj: I don't believe him. Remember the last time he was there was to speak about that property, right? I hope he was there again for the same reason.

Ashwathy: My father is a person who has a clear vision about what he wants to do. He does not jump up and down as you do.

Shinoj: Does he have any intentions of registering that property with Manojan after he has kids?

Ashwathy runs her fingers through her untied hair rolling up closer to Shinoj says.

Ashwathy: That's true. That's why I always doubt the father and mother asking me to speak to Surabhi about having a baby.

Shinoj: Aah! you've got it now, this matter needs a lot of thinking. Let's discuss it together.. You too come with me...

Shinoj is turning off the lights. Taking no notice of his blanket lying on the bed, he purposely rolls inside Ashwathy's blanket to caress her, and the scene fades to black.

CHAPTER 37

PEDOPHOBIA

Day/Int.

The scene opens with an establishing shot of the small cafeteria on a cool Sunday evening, showing the dimly lit interior with a few tables and chairs occupied by people enjoying their evening snacks. The camera then zooms in to focus on Manojan and Sumesh, who are sitting next to each other.

Here comes Dr. Shanawaz. Sumesh gets up to see the doctor, and Manojan follows him with respect.

Dr. Shanawaz: Hello Sumesh, am I late?

The doctor smiles at Manojan and feels comfortable sitting in the opposite chair.

Doctor: Manojan, right? Sukumaran had told me about you and that is why I said it would be better if we met in public than in my private clinic. That will be a change for me too.

Manojan looks at Sumesh clueless while Dr. Shanawaz to Sumesh says

Shanawaz: If you don't mind, I want to talk to Manojan personally for five minutes.

Sumesh: Ok, sure, You people can carry on, I shall move away

While Sumesh gets up, Manojan looks at Sumesh and the doctor confused

Shanawaz: Look Manojan, This is not a counseling, just consider this as a friendly gesture

Manojan: But doctor, for that I don't have any……

Manojan looks at Sumesh. Sumesh signs for him to share his problem with the doctor.

Shanawaz: Manojan, I hope you haven't understood the importance of children in our lives.

Manojan is perplexed, and they are both staring at each other in confusion.

Shanawaz: If we understand that, it will actually change the way we live, we'll see things from new perspectives and hear something delightful that we haven't heard before.

To be transparent, there are many different types of phobias like, fearful of becoming a parent, hatred towards children, suspicious of raising a kid, etc. It's a kind of anxiety and we call it pedophobia or parenthood phobia.

Manojan must be surprised, why am I saying this? Surabhi Teacher is my daughter Surumi's class teacher. Dr. Shifali, my wife, had told me about talking to your wife. You might have guessed by now, why am I here?. Well, you both can visit my clinic sometime.

Manojan nods, still baffled and with many thoughts—he wins races with his thoughts. The doctor gets up and walks towards the door while Manojan looks at Sumesh. The camera slowly zooms away from the two friends as they sit in silence.

CHAPTER 38

A Beer

Night/Int.

The camera pans from the moonlit sky to the gate of Cheriyanddi Plackals' house, where Manojan walks into the darkness. As he approaches the front door, the camera shifts to a close-up shot of his hand reaching for the doorknob. The camera then moves to a medium shot of Manojan entering the house, revealing the warm light from inside.

Vijayan, after his dinner, was about to go to sleep while Manojan went inside his room without looking into Surabhi's face, who came out looking for him.

Manojan takes off his shirt and pulls out a towel from the hanger to take a bath. Manojan, disturbed and enraged, whispers to Surabhi.

Have you all decided to declare it to the world? I thought at least Surabhi will stand by my side.

Surabhi: What happened, Manojetta?

Manojan: When he told me about you, going to see the doctor, I was shocked.

Surabhi: What doctor, which doctor?

Manojan: The Doctor, mother of a student studying in your school. You could have told me, and if you wanted, we could have gone together.

Surabhi: She had met me the other day at school. When Susamma teacher asked me, I just told her but not much in greater detail.

Manojan: That was enough! That doctor went home and told her husband.

Surabhi: I just asked, Shifali doctor some questions to clarify. That's all.

Manojan: Do you drink?

Manojan receives a shocked stare from Surabhi before she speaks.

Surabhi: Me? Drink?

Manojan: Yeah...stuff like beer.

Surabhi: I had a beer only once, that too, in a wedding. That day even you were beside me. Why are you asking about that now?

As he leaves, Manojan turns around to face her and says

Manojan: That too is a reason.

The camera focuses on Surabhi's face as tears roll down her cheeks when he asks an unexpected question and behaves rudely, capturing her pain and heartbreak. It then pans over to Manojan's back as he walks away, symbolizing his emotional distance from Surabhi. Finally, a wide shot shows Surabhi alone in the empty room, highlighting her loneliness.

CHAPTER 39

HEAVY COMPENSATION

Day/Int.

At William lawyer's office, William lawyer is sitting on his chair with his lawyer coat hung on a bronze hanger on the wall right behind him.

As Vijayan sits across from William's lawyer, the camera pans to an insert shot of his close-up, then pulls back to show the full shot of Vijayan looking anxious and uneasy as he awaits the lawyer's move.

William lawyer, hands over a document to his assistant, who is seated very next to him on a wooden chair. When William lawyer asks the assistant to read it out loud,

Assistant: Vijayan, Cheriyandi Plakkal house, Vellarikund,

Sir,

I live on the land my ancestors left me., I've been renting out pandals for the past 40 years. Now I am willing to hand over this property of 10 cents land and the pandal warehouse attached to it to my only son, Cheriyandiplackal Manojan, to run his event management company and nut export business as per his wish...

William lawyer interrupts the assistant in between

William lawyer: O dude, make sure you write down the right word; it's a cashew nut, not just any nut. It has to be presented to the court.

Assistant: Sorry Sir.

William Advocate: Just leave it, correct it as nuts only. What do you say, Vijaya? … Okay you continue

Assistant: "… However, he must give my wife and I a grandchild within a year in exchange for this. Failing which he shall be liable to pay me back the entire amount I have spent on his upbringing till this day including the expenses of his wedding and honeymoon.

Also compensation for the insult and abandonment that we have to face from society for not having grandchildren, moreover…

Vijayan slowly raising up his right hand signals the assistant lawyer to stop reading and turns up to William lawyer

Vijayan: But lawyer, how will this.....?

William lawyer pulls out the document from his assistant and says to Vijayan

William lawyer: It's not just that. On these grounds, the total compensation includes all the mental agony you and your wife have been through….

William's lawyer returns his gaze to Vijayan, who is still perplexed and pondering William's words.

William lawyer: We will decide about the amount later. Now the amount shall multiply as he is taking his salary, right?

Vijayan: Yeah! He does

William lawyer: Then no problem. Moreover, he also has an income out of the nut business too. The case will hold strong.

Assistant: Sir, along with Manojan, his wife should also be added as a party of mental cruelty.

Vijayan: But Lawyer, don't you think it is too much to drag my daughter in law into it.

Once looking at Vijayan, William Advocate responded to his assistant with a deft smile and said:

It won't work with only one person, based on my past assistance.

Assistant lawyer looks up to William lawyer in pride and says

Assistant: If this is not enough, then we will add some more points like a violation of rights to become grandparents…

The assistant lawyer again looks up to William lawyer, and collects all his case files on the table getting ready to move out while William to Vijayan

William: Anyways, You just come, whenever I call you.

As William lawyer, and his assistant walk out of the cabin in a hurry, the camera shifts to a point-of-view shot from Vijayan's perspective. Vijayan still stands there, confused, for one last time before walking out of the office. The camera lingers on this shot for a moment.

CHAPTER 40

NO CHILD

Day/Ext.

Surabhi walks down the street, her shoulders slumped and her head hanging low. The camera captures her from a low angle, emphasizing her dejected posture. As Surabhi walks towards Suja and Sonumon, the camera zooms in on their happy faces, which stand out in contrast to Surabhi's sad expression. The background score changes from somber to upbeat, creating a sense of hope and positivity. As Suja and Sonumon talk to Surabhi, the camera moves to a medium shot,

Suja: Don't be sad, I do understand. Sumeshettan was saying to me, No one had ever expected Vijayettan would bring such a case against Manojettan.

Surabhi Teacher: What else could I say? Maalu had called twice to ask about this. What should I say to each of them?

Suja: The three of us have studied together and are the same age. I have a kid. Maybe Vijayettan is upset with him because he doesn't have one.

Surabhi seemed reluctant to discuss it further. She smiles at Suja's child as they walk away. As Surabhi walks away, the camera cuts to a close-up shot of Sonumon's face. His bright smile fills the frame, radiating pure joy and positivity.

CHAPTER 41

'FATHERS'

Day/Int.

The camera captures a low-angle shot of Manojan as he climbs up the wooden stairs leading to William Lawyer's office. The camera slowly pans up to show his sweaty face and his quick movements. The angle emphasizes Manojan's urgency and determination. With each step, the sound of his footsteps echoes through the empty stairwell, adding a sense of urgency and tension to the scene.

He pretends to be clearly ignoring William lawyer and walks away towards Wilson lawyer's cabin, entering with a deep breath and calming down in front of Wilson lawyer

Wilson lawyer: Manoja, sit down and relax. Would you like some water?

Wilson lawyer hands him a bottle of water, but Manojan clearly denies it and continues.

Manojan: I didn't come here to drink water; instead, I came to make them too.

Wilson lawyer: Do not worry, Manoja; I will handle things. Look, we had studied LLB together, so, you know about the counter-petition, right? We will file that.

Manojan: You do whatever you want but I know how to tackle this. The issue is that I haven't been familiar with laws and codes in recent years.

Wilson: You want your father to lose, don't you?

Manojan: Yes, but don't let your father win. if he wins indirectly my father wins. Our fathers shouldn't win anyway.

The same Assistant lawyer who was helping William Advocate slowly walks without anybody noticing and stands in a corner while Wilson sits there on a chair

Wilson: No.., fathers shouldn't win. We'll argue that you're infertile and so unable to have children. Who will win?

Assistant: We will win... If that is insufficient, we will include additional legal provisions to strengthen the argument.

The assistant lawyer looks back at Wilson lawyer with pride.

Wilson: Ok, I'll call you when I do, so come down then.

As Manojan stands up, the camera shifts from a two-shot of him and Wilson to a single eye-level shot of Manojan's determined face. His eyes are narrowed with frustration as he turns towards Wilson before storming out of the room. The camera lingers on his face for a moment, emphasizing the intensity of his emotions,

Manojan: Fathers...

Wilson lawyer: … Will never win... Is that enough?

CHAPTER 42

A Decision

Day/Int.

The camera is positioned at a medium shot level, capturing Sumithramma sitting on the steps beside the cowshed in the backyard with the midday sun shining in the background. The shot should emphasize the peacefulness of the moment and the tranquility of the surroundings.

She is combing Maalu's hair. Maalu's husband, Girish, is playing with the child in the yard.

Sumithramma: Good to see you people come home, You know the situation here, right? Did you speak to Surabhi about Manojan?

Maalu: She is also saying the same thing. There is nothing wrong with Manojettan.

Meanwhile, Manojan, riding his bike, enters the warehouse with Pandal material. Maalu quickly turned around and asked Manojan as he looked at her.

Maalu: Chetta, What do you think you're doing?

Manojan gets off the bike, stares back at her, and says

Manojan: You should have asked the same question to Achchan

Maalu: I am not supporting anyone, but...

Manojan: Yes. But you haven't listened to my side of the story.

While removing the items from the bike, he stares at Maalu's child as she plays, then continues.

Manojan: When the children are small, everyone loves them. But the problem starts when they grow up. Only then do people speak about daily expenses, calculations and they will even interfere in personal matters.

Maalu: In which personal matter of yours did Achchan interfere...

Manojan: Look, I am clear, I don't want to raise a kid the way Achchan raised me as per their wish. That's my decision.

Girish silently listens to all the conversation but doesn't make any move

Maalu: Ok, What about Surabhi? Has she also decided the same?

Sumithramma: Stop it both of you.

Manojan: Anyways, What Achchan did, has come as a boon to me. At least now I can open up about everything.

Amma, serve me food.

CHAPTER 43

FORGIVE ME 'ACHCHA'

Eve./Int.

A night shot opens with the moon shining bright in the dark sky, casting a dim light on the Cheriyandi Plakkal house. Sumithramma, Ashwathy, and Shinoj are sitting in the verandah, their silhouettes visible against the moonlit background.

The children's games and the TV volume could be heard from inside. Inside the room, Surabhi is making corrections to the exam papers.

Ashwathy: We couldn't come last week, but had planned to come this Saturday. What to do, we had to rush because of the situation.

Sumithramma: Good that you are here, I don't have peace of mind. My fear is, what's going to happen next.

Shinoj: Don't be afraid, Amme Aliyan is not a troublemaker. But Achchan is one...

Vijayan comes there; the TV is still playing from inside. While Ashwathy is looking at her father, she asks Sumithramma.

Ashwathy: Amme, you ask Achchan in front of us.

Sumithramma: Why were you late this evening?

Vijayan: I had gone to see that William lawyer.

Sumithramma: I can't understand anything, now everyone has started asking me about the matter. What should I say?

Vijayan: Didn't we discuss this before going forward?

Ashwathy: Achcha, you could have asked us too before doing all this, isn't it Shinojetta?

Vijayan: I didn't feel the need to ask you.

Shinoj: It is always like that, Achchan doesn't love us the way we love, you are always partial towards us. You may still have shown some respect to the Karnataka Police. No, not for me.

Vijayan: It wasn't just me complaining about that. Everyone complained, didn't it?

Shinoj looks at Surabhi coming out of her room.

Shinoj: Hey! Not at all. No one has any complaint against Manojanaliyan...

As Vijayan stands up to walk towards his room, he gets a message on his phone. Vijayan receives an audio clip from Manojan via WhatsApp. He does have a startling look when he plays the audio in front of everyone.

'beep'

Manojan (vo): 'Achcha, You have done something which no father will ever do to his son. Hence, I will also do something that no son will ever do to his father..

'beep'

I have decided to file a case against you for giving me birth without my permission. "Forgive me Achcha".

'beep'

The family members looked at each other in shock as they heard Manojan's words. The camera zooms in on their surprised faces, capturing the mix of emotions.

CHAPTER 44

'That's All Your Honour'

Morning/Ext.

The expansive grounds of the magistrate court are seen in the established shot, which is taken from a top angle. The buildings are painted in shades of beige and brown, with a large sign board indicating the name of the court. Several cars and motorcycles are parked haphazardly, indicating a busy Monday around 10 a.m.

A rooster out of nowhere suddenly runs helter-skelter around the premises of the court. The camera zooms in on the rooster as it runs around the magistrate court compound. Its feathers are ruffled, and its bright red comb bounces with each step. Its sharp talons scratch at the ground as it darts back and forth.

Two policemen, one has a large belly, whereas the other is slim and Three court staff in Mundu (Lungi) are chasing the rooster. and a few bystanders are laughing at their plight. The rooster then flies into the police jeep parked near the compound and poops on the seat.

Manojan rides on his bike inside the court compound, and the rooster is flying high with much spirit after the poop, directly on Manojan's bike fuel tank. Manojan gets startled by the bird's sudden attack, and he loses control, and the bike skids.

Court officials run against the rooster and capture the accused while police officers pant, and Manojan and his bike fall to the ground.

Court employee: Sorry Sir, When the Magistrate has himself ordered us, we have to do it. We have started this chase since morning. The rooster disturbed the court proceeding, that's the case.

Manojan looks totally confused at the policeman who is standing in front of him, panting with a sweaty face. The policeman then takes the rooster from the court employee's hand and speaks.

Thank you, sir, thank you very much. An FIR has been registered against this accused, that's why we were behind this. Hope you are fine?

The court staff and the police walk towards the court, holding the rooster.

Dissolve to

Manojan enters the court. Vijayan and William lawyer, are sitting on the bench. Wilson comes to Manojan and says

Wilson lawyer: The next case to be called is ours. I'll let you know. Take a seat.

Cut to

An employee is holding the rooster and standing near the witness box. The magistrate observes the rooster. Under the magistrate's desk, a court attendant gets up and reads the case.

Under doubtful circumstances, a rooster, whose owner is not known yet, entered the court premises during working hours and disturbed the court proceedings. As the employees have informed, under section CRPC 102, the trial will go on, and the consent under the court is informed regarding this.

Magistrate: So… At last it is caught... Confessed...isn't it?

Employee: Yes Sir.

Magistrate: This thing is not worth Rs.500 and since it is a living being, it's difficult to keep it in court. Hence, it shall be auctioned. How about that?

Employee: The owner of the rooster is here, Sir.

Magistrate: Ah.! then no need to auction, hand over the rooster to him.

The employee gracefully hands over the rooster to the owner, and the magistrate looks solemnly at the owner and says.

Magistrate: Now onwards if I see this rooster inside the court premises or the courtroom and disturbs, poops, or crows, the owner of the rooster will be fully responsible... Did you understand?

Owner: Okay sir, but there is a problem… In the daylight, this rooster is blind.

Magistrate: If it's blind, then get it treated mister.., or cage it, Even if you are still unable to manage it, use Kerala spices to make a curry out of it.

Dissolve to

As the judge makes a joke, all those present in court start to laugh. As the court attendant called out the case number and William advocate walked to the front, the courtroom erupted in laughter.

William Advocate: For their peaceful mental pleasure and to be happily passing time in old age, my clients, Mr. Cheriyandi Plakkal Vijayan and his wife Sumithramma need a grandchild from their son Manojan and his wife Surabhi within one year.

William the lawyer continues to speak as the magistrate, who is perplexed by what is happening, scratches his chin. William advocate continues.

Your Honour! For the past 6 years, my clients have been going through mental agony, emotional pressure, and domestic violence. Hence, if the said condition is not accepted by the opposite party, In such case the amount spent to raise their son, educate him, and get him married including the honeymoon expenses should be paid back with interest.

Since it is a fundamental right of any human being to live in peace without any mental torture as it's violated by the opposite party. And finally, before they die, they just want to see at least one grandchild… That's all Your Honour.

The magistrate continues to stare at both parties while resting his hand on his chin. He finally speaks up, taking a deep breath.

Magistrate: See William lawyer, why to bother the court for these silly matters; they may be resolved at home.

William Advocate: No Your honor… This is not a silly matter… This is an infringement of rights. It is a dream of every parent to become a grandparent and They had been waiting for years to become grandparents…, your honor.

Wilson defended his father's stance by responding to it.

Wilson Advocate: Your honour, My client, Mr. Manojan, was brought into this world by the opposite party, Mr. Vijayan, without his consent; that is the root cause of all these problems.

Even now, decades after his birth, he is subjected to mental harassment; additionally, as a child, he was tortured by the opposing party through domestic abuse and strict rules.

Because of all these things, my client has started hating children and childhood, being afraid of children, and whatnot. Your honour, this means he has been suffering in this manner for the past 38 long years. That's all there is to it, your honor.

With his palm on his chin, the magistrate is still seated in the same posture as previously.

Magistrate: This could be one of the first unique cases in the history of Kerala. The rarest of the rare. Isn't it William advocate? Therefore, this judiciary needs much more time to conclude on this. I can only follow the book of law. We shall only consider the case after the vacation. Is that ok?

CHAPTER 45

Bloody Villagers

Night/Ext.

On the eve of a lavish wedding day. The camera pans from the ground up. The colorful, bright lights have been lit by the neighborhood, and loud, funky music is being played on speakers.

Manojan is giving instructions to the workers erecting the pandal, while Babu, as usual, is pretending to be busy and just running up and down the open area.

Two fat middle-aged ladies in brightly coloured sarees sit on the chairs, chopping the vegetables, giggling, and chatting to themselves while listening to music.

Lady 1: We need a tube light here, isn't it yettaththiye (sister)?

Lady 2: You see that guy? We can ask him

Lady 2 pointing out at Manojan slowly whispers

Lady 2: Do you realize who that person is? Vijayettan's son. The guy who does that nut business.

Lady 1: Of course, how can I forget Vijayettan? He had come to see me before he got married to Sumithra.

Lady 2: Lucky that you didn't marry that nut, or else you would have delivered such a Nutty Manojan

Lady 1: Hey.. Don't talk about Vijayettan is a Nut..this guy.. So he's the one who filed a case against Vijayettan and dragged him to court. He looks like a dimwit. A flickering Tubelight..

Both of them are laughing as the vegetable is still being sliced.

Gopi, the son of the lady who asked for the tubelight, comes to her in an inebriated state after having a few pegs with his friends and blabbers.

Hey! Mother, listen to me. Haven't I told you a million times not to just attend a wedding without being invited? And talking about me... You just insult me. Anyway I am leaving.

Dissolve to

Sonumon, along with the other two little boys, is running around the yard with papers and flowers in their hands, throwing them around as the ladies laugh at their naughtiness.

Manojan is giving instructions to the workers and is helping Babu, who is decorating the pandal. Ladies and the invitees are speaking to themselves, laughing, and enjoying the ambience since the song on the speakers is being played loudly, Sumesh yells at Manojan,

Sumesh: Eda, you could have told me before taking such a step. Everybody believes that you are the one who file a case against your father.

The song is playing a little more loudly on the speakers, and Manojan replies to Sumesh in a louder voice.

Manojan: What should I have asked you about it? Allow the villagers to speak behind my back if they want to.

As Manojan uttered these lines, the song stopped suddenly, and it was obvious that everyone in the neighborhood understood what Manojan was attempting to say to Sumesh.

Manojan: If you have come to speak to me on behalf of my father? Then you should better understand, I will not let my father win at any cost by having children. Yes, I filed the case against him. Bloody villagers! We shall solve this in court.

The villagers exchange puzzled looks as they listen to Manojan. The camera zooms in on Sonumon's hand as he presses the music button. Sonumon is seen in the center of the shot smiling and enjoying, then presses the music button again while the high-groovy music fills the open yard.

CHAPTER 46

The Whole Town Knows

Night/Int.

The camera slowly pans up to show Sumithramma's tired face as she prepares to settle into bed after a long day. A low angle shot captures Sumithramma's hand reaching into the cupboard to grab a fresh pillow cover and tries to change the ones on the bed while Vijayan, deeply looking down at his mobile, keeps scrolling up the display.

Sumithramma: What do you mean by this? What's your intention?

Vijayan: What? hey..This is not what you are thinking.

Vijayan switches off his mobile display and keeps it on the side table.

Sumithramma: The whole town knows about it. Have you ever heard of anything like this in the world?

Vijayan: Before you signed the document, I asked you, right?

Sumithramma: Somehow if you can solve and finish it off, it will be of great help. At least I can sleep in peace.

Vijayan: It's not just me, He should also think and decide about that.

Sumithramma: What should he decide? Do you think these things could be done by filing a case?

Vijayan: Aah! We shall wait and watch.

Sumithramma: People tend to assume that there is something wrong with him.

Vijayan: There is nothing wrong with him. Those people also know that. You try to catch some sleep.

CHAPTER 47

A Return Case

Eve./Int.

The camera is positioned at Surabhi's eye level, capturing the deep emotion in her eyes as she sits on the bed in their bedroom. The dimly lit room creates an atmosphere of somberness and tension.

Manojan is seated next to her, looking down and avoiding eye contact. Surabhi takes a deep breath before finally mustering up the courage to speak.

The silence in the room is palpable as she tries to convince Manojan to open up and talk to her. The ambiance is heavy with unresolved issues and unspoken words, as Surabhi struggles to connect with her husband.

Surabhi: What Achchan and Amma are saying is also right, isn't Manojetta?

Manojan: What could be wrong with filing a return case if what they did was right?

Surabhi moves near Manojan trying to convince him

Surabhi: Not that Manojetta when we call it a family, aren't children a part of it?

When Manojan looks at Surabhi, she makes a sad face.

Surabhi: I never said I don't want children. I just said I didn't want it immediately after marriage so I can complete my training

period at school. I was just waiting for that training period to get over. I always thought you were doing all this because of your anger towards your father.

A medium-close-up shot of Surabhi and Manojan's hands, with the camera positioned slightly above their hands to show Surabhi's gentle pressing action.

Dissolve to

Surabhi gets a call on her mobile from Maalu and picks it up

Maalu: Surabhi, we are always with you when you need us. When my parents came to know about me and Girishettan's love. Manojettan was the only one who stood by our side... and you are among my friends. We can never forget that. Convince him, Surabhi, and you both should go to the doctor tomorrow. Goodnight.

A close-up shot of Surabhi's face, with the background blurred out to emphasize her emotions.

CHAPTER 48

SILENCE!

Day/Int.

It's a fresh new day before the tiring court session begins. A low angle shot shows Vijayan standing in the busy court corridor. In the background, the imposing building of the court stands tall, with the morning sun casting a warm glow on its walls.

The sounds of shuffling papers, footsteps, and muffled voices can be heard in the background, creating a sense of hustle and bustle.

Vijayan is looking all around as if he's searching for someone in the crowd. William looks at Vijayan from the far end and approaches him.

William Lawyer: Vijaya, what are you looking for, me?

Vijayan: Lawyere, Manojan hasn't come yet?

William Lawyer: Hayye...!! Are you here in the court to see your sweet son?

Vijayan: I didn't get to see him at home nowadays, that's why?

William Lawyer: Look Vijayan, The whole of Kerala state is looking forward to hearing this case. You know people are extremely anxious about the outcome of this case. Come fast.. They will be calling our case soon.

At the same time, at the end of the court corridor, Manojan and Wilson Lawyer walk in hurriedly and enter the courtroom. Vijayan looks at Manojan on the pretext of not looking at him directly.

The court officer in uniform calls the case number while the junior magistrate hands over the file to the magistrate on the dais. The magistrate opens the file, reads a few lines, and pauses without looking up.

Magistrate: Both the Father and the Son are here, right?

The magistrate looks up at Vijayan and Manojan, stroking up his spectacles with his left hand, and takes a look at both advocates.

Magistrate: You could have called them up for a compromise and settled the case, couldn't you? Why bother the court and the preceding?

William Lawyer: Sorry your honour! This is a case that the whole state is looking up to. Moreover, Vijayan is hugely respected as a socially responsible person, so..

Magistrate:..So, the court needs some more time to settle this.

Manojan, who is innocently standing on the other side, is folding his hands. The magistrate looks up at all the advocates lined up in front of him and finally, stroking his pen once on the table, says:

Magistrate: Give some time for everything… It doesn't take much time to have children... isn't it?

The people inside the courtroom laughed, looking at each other's faces over a satirical joke from the magistrate. Vijayan and Manojan, too, look at each other as they contemplate their fates in the courtroom and put their heads down while the magistrate calls out.

Silence !

CHAPTER 49

QUALITY NUT 'LLB'

Morning/Int.

The camera is positioned low, almost at ground level, as Babu begins his day by carefully picking up the cashew nuts scattered on the mat inside the verandah.

The gentle rustling of the cashew nuts mixes with the sounds of birds chirping in the background, creating a peaceful and tranquil atmosphere.

Manojan comes out of the house and looks down at Babu, while Babu, holding a few comparatively small cashew nuts out of the heap in his hand, asks innocently.

Babu: Saab, ye small nuts kidar rakhne ka?

He always asks illogical questions, which annoys Manojan.

Manojan: You can throw it wherever you want.

Babu, uncertain of what Manojan meant, looks at him with a blank expression on his face. Babu, realizing that Manojan is angry, slowly slips the cashew nut into his mouth. Manojan piles up the cashew nut packets in a hurry.

Babu: Woh Purushan bhai bol raha tha, all your nuts are of the same quality.

Manojan piles up the packets; he gets angry listening to this feedback and immediately shouts.

Manojan: You… Kya kar raha tha... da here? I have told you many times not to eat nuts while packing.

Babu: Apne abhi bhola dhana, You throw it wherever you want.

Cut to

When Manojan enters the house, he grumbles at him because he is worried about getting Babu right on every job. Manojan cools down when Sumithramma serves him Puttu and Kadala curry on the dining table.

Vijayan comes there to have breakfast, and Manojan, looking at Vijayan, immediately gets up and walks to the wash basin.

Sumithramma: Why don't you finish this?

Manojan: Enough…

Vijayan stares at Manojan, who ignores him, and Manojan, looking into the mirror above the wash basin, washes his hands and murmurs.

Manojan: He might file any other case of having more Puttu's. Anyways, for society, I am the one who filed the case against him, right?

Vijayan looks at Sumithramma and says

Vijayan: Our advocate William…

Manojan: … Our Advocate? How come our advocate? He is your advocate, not mine. My advocate is Wilson Advocate. Everyone knows what are you up to?

Ready to leave for school wearing a saree, Surabhi packs up a lunch box in the kitchen.

Sumithramma: Can you both stop this?

Manojan: Why should I stop? I have been served a notice including the fees he had paid for my LLB. So let me show you all the advantages of learning the same LLB....

Surabhi comes out of the kitchen with the lunch box in her hand.

Manojan: Surabhi, Keep that food there…

Surabhi is distressed as she looks at Sumithramma.

Sumithramma: Have you gone mad?

Manojan: Yes! I am mad. That's why I went to the doctor. You all know that right?

Surabhi, I am telling you, keep that tiffin box there.

Surabhi stands there helplessly. Babu arrives with a few whole, clean, jumbo cashew nuts in hand, unaware of the gravity of the situation for Manojan.

Babu: Yeh bada andi (nut) kaun se packet mey..?

The camera focuses on Manojan's face as he angrily stares at Babu. Suddenly, the camera switches to a close-up shot of Babu's hand, Manojan slaps Babu's hand, which Manojan slaps, causing the cashew nuts to fly in the air. Babu searches for the cashew nut everywhere.

Cut to a shot of Sumithramma and Surabhi, who look frightened and shocked by Manojan's outburst. The background music intensifies with each passing second.

As Babu leaves in disappointment, the camera zooms in on the large cashew nut lying close to the verandah door. The background music grows more intense as the camera focuses on the cashew nut, seemingly insignificant but a symbol of the tension and conflict brewing within.

The camera slowly pans out to show the worried and fearful faces of Sumithramma and Surabhi, as they brace themselves for what may come next. The tension in the air is palpable as the scene ends.

CHAPTER 50

PUKE

Eve./Int.

The camera is positioned on the gate as it slowly creaks open, revealing the dimly lit compound with Surabhi and Sumithramma sitting on the verandah.

The sound of Manojan's bike engine grows louder as he approaches, adding to the tension in the air. The camera then pans to Surabhi and Sumithramma as they turn their heads towards the gate, their faces etched with worry and anticipation.

Manojan's bike enters the gate. Looking at the bike coming to a halt, feeling uneasy, Sumithramma and Surabhi walk up to Manojan while he completely ignores them, and Sumithramma speaks up.

Sumithramma: You change and come, I will serve you dinner

Maniojan: No need, I ate outside

Surabhi goes to him and calmly says

Surabhi: Please have dinner

Manojan: Didn't I tell you, I don't want to eat

His response makes Surabhi and Sumithramma sad, and they both walk to the kitchen.

Cut to

Manojan is sitting in the bedroom and Surabhi comes inside, standing near the window slowly tells Manojan

Surabhi: Tomorrow is Saturday, can you drop me to my house after school

Manojan looks up to Surabhi and asks

Manojan: And then..., did you think I would be lonely?

Surabhi: No, it's not like that. It's been a long time since I haven't been to my Mom's place. Shall we both go and stay there for 2 days?

After saying this, Surabhi feels a little weird, like she has the urge to vomit. She presses her hand towards her mouth and quickly walks outside the room, while Manojan immediately follows her.

Surabhi runs towards the wash basin in the dining hall and tries to puke. Sumithramma becomes agitated and runs to Surabhi, while Vijayan smirks at Sumithramma. Manojan looks at Vijayan and lowers his head while Sumithramma rubs Surabhi's back, trying to pacify her.

Manojan looks at Surabhi washing her face through the mirror. The camera begins with a medium shot of Manojan and Surabhi standing side by side at the sink, with a slightly blurred background. The lens is slightly zoomed in to emphasize their faces and the tension between them and cuts to behind Surabhi's reflection in the mirror.

In the background, as Vijayan walks past, he gives Manojan a dubious look before entering his room. The camera pans to follow him before zooming back to focus on Surabhi and Manojan's reflections once again.

The camera shifts its focus to Manojan with a quick new focal point of the shot, an extreme mid-shot of Manojan's eyes, Surabhi is the focus of Manojan's attention, and he repeatedly nods his head as though he has decided something.

Surabhi was becoming more frightened, and Manojan's attitude was getting more aggressive. The background music intensifies, building tension in the scene.

CHAPTER 51

Laugh Out Loud

Morning/Ext.

The camera captures the wide view of the local park, with the morning sun shining brightly over the lush green trees and grass. In the distance, a group of energetic old men can be seen gathered in a circle, their hands clapping rhythmically as they participate in the laughing club.

The sound of their laughter echoes through the park, creating a lively and cheerful atmosphere. The background music is a lively and upbeat tune, adding to the overall energy and vibrancy.

As the camera pans in on the group, William Advocate and Vijayan can be seen. Capture their happy faces and bright smiles as they enjoy the morning exercise routine. After a few minutes of continuous clapping, Vijayan and William Advocate walk towards a bench nearby.

Vijayan: I am not able to laugh out loud, Lawyere.

William Advocate: But you were the one who laughed out loud today right.

Vijayan: If Surabhi delivers a baby within a year, then I shall have to register that 10 cents in his name, isn't it Advocate?

William Advocate: If at all, only if she delivers within a year, that's it.

Vijayan worried with what happened last night looks at William Advocate and says

Vijayan: Lawyere, My Daughter-in-law vomited last night,

William Advocate looks at Vijayan perplexed and with eyes wide open

William Advocate: How many times?

The member of the laughing club continue to laugh loudly clapping their hands as this irritates Vijayan even more

Vijayan: Lawyere, Does that really matter, how many times? But what about the case now...can we…?

The camera begins with a medium close-up of William's face as he speaks, with a puzzled expression on his face.

William Advocate: Wait a minute, Are you saying we should drop the case? Do you know the serious complications involved? She had just vomited, right? What does her vomiting have to do with the case? I really doubt it's his new plan, I really don't believe him, since he is your son.

As he finishes, the camera shifts to a close-up of his eyes, which have a cunning glint in them. Finally, the camera zooms out to a wide shot of the park, capturing both William and Vijayan's body language as they continue their conversation.

CHAPTER 52

A Quick life Saver

Day/Int.

Surabhi had gone to her mother's place for a few days, Sumithramma and Vijayan had gone to a nearby village to attend a noolukettu, a tradition of tying a black thread around the baby's waist on the 28th day after birth. It's unusual for the "Cheriyanddi Plackal" to feel empty for so long with only Manojan.

Manojan walks into the kitchen at noon and calls up Sumithramma after attempting to cook something for lunch

Manojan: Amme, I want to make an omelet.

Sumithramma: So what? The eggs are lying in the fridge.

Manojan: After pouring oil, I just need to break the eggs and put it on the pan, isn't it?

Sumithramma: Umm...! It's not just that, add some pepper and salt too. Adding some green chilies and tomatoes would taste better. Rice is kept in the bowl with the lid closed in the corner. Heat it up if required.

Manojan: No need, I don't have time for that.

Dissolve to

Manojan carries some rice and his freshly cooked new invention on a plate towards the dining table. A yellow tennis ball flies into his compound, followed by Sonumon, who, after a few seconds, pushes the main gate to take back his ball.

While he tries to take the ball, it slips again and falls a little further. The child goes after it.

The yellow ball lands on the verandah of Manojan's house. Manojan is eating when he hears a noise and walks out to see Sonumon playing.

Manojan, frustrated seeing the child in their house in a panic state, shouts **Sumeshe.... Sumeshe.....Suje... Suje...** with no response from any one of them nearby.

Manojan runs inside, realizing that no one is listening. A panicked Manojan eats the rice in a hurry, Sonumon heartily smiling at him.

Sonu looks at the few toys (Prasoon's and Prabhi's) lying around and happily starts playing with them. Sonumon also notices the small, colourful Lego plastic building blocks near the main door of the verandah. He continues to play with it until he finds something more interesting. He picks it up and puts it in his mouth.

While coming out Manojan saw Sonumon gasping for breath. Manojan sees the child struggling and he gets frightened. Very irritated not knowing what to do, he screams at the top of his voice **Amma... Amme... Sumeshe.......**

Realizing that nobody is there for his help. Manojan comes to the child and pats his head and back, screaming for help.

There is a strong sense of tension as he realises how serious the situation is. The camera then shifts to a close-up of the child's face, who is still gasping for air, his eyes pleading for help.

Manojan gains some courage and puts his finger inside the child's mouth to slowly pull out the thing stuck in his mouth. His hands begin to shake as he realizes the gravity of the situation. The camera angle changes to a low-angle shot, emphasizing Manojan's determination and courage to save the child's life.

The camera zooms in on Manojan's face as he is shocked to see the thing stuck in his fingertips—a jumbo cashew nut! The music starts to build up, adding to the tension of the scene. Suddenly, the camera cuts to a close-up shot of the child's face as he starts to choke again. Sonumon faints due to a lack of oxygen, and Manojan immediately carries the child outside the house on his shoulder, crying for help.

CHAPTER 53

I.C.U

Day/Int.

The camera slowly zooms in on Sonumon's face, revealing the worry lines etched deep into his forehead. His face is covered with a transparent oxygen mask connected to a large cylinder chained beside his bed in the Government Hospital ICU. The beeping of the various medical equipment echoes throughout the room, punctuating the otherwise silent and sterile atmosphere.

The doctor is examining Sonumon and instructing the two nurses who are standing behind him with a crash cart, some files, and Medicaid. Suja is depressed and standing outside the ICU, waiting for the doctor.

Doctor comes out of the ICU while, at the same time, Manojan walks in the corridor; he walks into the ICU door in front of Doctor and feels guilty.

Doctor: There is an injury deep below his throat, an abrasion. We will keep him under observation for the next 48 hours. Let's wait.

Manojan's face shows a mix of emotions - sadness, guilt, and helplessness. He knows he is responsible for Sonumon's condition Manojan looks at Sonumon through the ICU glass window. His gaze shifts to Suja, her face pale and her eyes brimming with tears. Manojan can feel her pain. He looks back at Sonumon.

CHAPTER 54

Posco

Day/Ext.

On a bright and sunny day, the camera shows an exterior shot of the police station building, The shot slowly zooms in to show Manojan sitting on a bench in the verandah. He looks nervous and fidgety, constantly glancing around at the other people in the station. The camera angle changes to a close-up of Manojan's face, showing beads of sweat on his forehead.

Inside the station, a policeman in civil dress stood in front of Sub-Inspector Jnanasheelan, listening to him carefully.

Outside the police station, some people are standing in a group with Prafullan, Kunjhettan, and Purushan. Shinoj in a civil dress comes out of the police station hurriedly, stands near the side door, and looks around. Purushan comes to Shinoj in a hurry.

Purushan: Sir, don't ever consider your relationship with him, don't miss this golden opportunity, just be specific that he is a nuisance to the society.

Shinoj looks at Prafullan and Kunjettan and lowers his voice.

Shinoj: Just make sure you sell that property at all costs; I won't be able to breathe easily until then.

Purushan: Sir, just fix him under a police case and I shall take care of the rest.

A policeman comes out of S.I. 's cabin and tells Manojan to come inside. Looking at that, Shinoj comes running to Manojan.

Shinoj: Dear, Just agree with whatever S.I has to say with your mouth shut. Don't just throw your senseless law points at him

Manojan looks at Shinoj and walks inside, and Shinoj follows him inside. Manojan stands in front of S.I. Jnanasheelan, while Shinoj stands behind Manojan. S.I. looks at Shinoj and says

S.I. Jnansheelan: What are you doing in this station? Go outside. Keep your influential power outside the state border.

Shinoj walks out, and S.I. Jnansheelan is looking at Manojan.

S.I.: What syndrome do you have? He has come up with a new syndrome which no one has ever heard of. If you stay behind bars for some time, Everything will be in place.

S.I. Jnansheelan comes very close to Manojan after standing up and looking at him angrily.

S.I.: What is your problem? You are doing this with an intention, isn't it?

S.I. Jnansheelan gives Manojan a tight slap on his chin. The unexpected slap brings in a lot of insults and pain Manojan feels miserable. S.I. to Manojan then rudely utters

S.I. Jnansheelan: Offense against children, POSCO Act, 11 and 12. Non-bailable, I hope you know codes better, right? How many times have you done this?

Prafullan, Kunjhettan, and Purushan peep at Manojan from the outside. Manojan sadly looks at them and says:

Manojan: Sir, I.....have not!

S.I. Jnansheelan asked a question while looking out the window.

S.I. Jnansheelan: So you mean, whatever happened that day at school wasn't your fault, Hmm! one thing I assure you if something happens to that child, I will make sure that you will land up in jail for lifetime. You understand that?

Manojan nods his head in agreement

S.I. Jnansheelan: How will you understand? You don't have a kid, right? That kid's parents came to me and pleaded, only that's the reason to let you go free now. Get out!

Manojan doesn't understand anything and slowly walks out, looking back once at S.I. Jnansheelan, who stares at him while the policeman at the entrance with a pen ready in his hands tells him.

Policeman: Sign here after writing your full name and address.

As he steps out into the open air, Manojan's eyes fill with tears, and his chin begins to tremble. He looks down at his feet and takes a deep breath, trying to steady his emotions. But the tears continue to flow down his face, and he wipes them away with the back of his hand.

Slowly, he makes his way down the steps of the police station, each step heavy with the weight of his sadness. The sounds of the bustling street fade away as he walks, lost in his thoughts and emotions.

CHAPTER 55

SECOND LIFE

Day/Ext.

After being shifted to a ward from the ICU, the child is still wearing an oxygen mask while his mother, Suja tense stands next to him. Manojan is standing a little away near the door of the ward. After examining the child, the doctor comes near the door and says,

Doctor: In such cases, parents are panicked and unsure what to do. That child is alive now, Just because of your quick, bold and timely action. I appreciate your braveness.

Manojan's eyes fill with tears when the doctor continues with a clear beam.

Doctor: Just think that this is the second birth you are giving to your son.

Manojan finds no words to express and looks at Suja

Manojan: Doctor! Sonumon...my son..he is..

Before Manojan could stop concluding, doctor pats Manojan on his shoulders and continues

Doctor: Ok. Take good care of him now onwards. We just live for our kids and they are the ones who make us feel complete? isn't?

As the doctor walks away, Manojan turns his gaze towards Sonumon, who is sleeping peacefully on the bed. As Manojan comes closer to Sonumon's bed, the camera follows him in a tracking shot while slowly adjusting the focus from Manojan to Sonumon's face. The camera then settles on Sonumon's peaceful expression.

The shot then switches to a close-up of Manojan's teary eyes as he looks down at the boy.

He realizes the strength and courage he possesses within himself and feels proud of it. The background music starts to pick up pace and become more upbeat; he has a determined look on his face.

The camera then zooms out to show Manojan sitting beside Sonumon's bed, his hand gently resting on the boy's arm. Then, with pride, Manojan sees his own hands.

CHAPTER 56

HEREDITARY

Morning/Int.

The sound of machines whirring and workers chatting fills the air as the camera pans across the cashew nut business operating out of a small shack in the countryside. Bags of cashews are stacked high, and workers are sorting and processing the nuts with skillful hands. The same two chubby middle-aged women are smashing roasted cashew nuts.

The fresh smell of burning cashews fills the air, and some cashews are scattered around. Manojan on his bike, with Babu as the pillion, rides through the scenic beauty of a small village a few kilometers away.

He frequently comes there to buy cashew nuts in bulk and put them under his label. He comes to a stop near a small home industry where a few ladies are frying cashew nuts along the shell and opening up the shells to separate them.

A few children are playing with the home-made wooden toys, laughing and cheering. Manojan sits back on his bike, and Babu approaches a lady to inquire about the cashew, while two fat middle-aged ladies observe Manojan's conversation.

Lady 1: yettaththiye (sister), does he buy nuts here?

Lady 2: Did he get out of the mess so quickly without being jailed?

During this moment, Babu approach the woman, and she asks,

Lady 1: Did you come to buy nuts?

Babu: Ha.. Manojettan... nuts...

Hearing his words, the ladies burst out laughing. Babu goes inside a small shed to check on the stock, while Manojan watches the children playing and observing this the lady says,

Lady 2: Look yettaththi, he is watching those kids

Lady 1: He seems like a, Child abuser

Lady 2: He has this disease of killing children

Have you heard of 'Lungi lifting disease'? Vijayettan's father Cashew**also had a similar kind of disease they say. Seems like hereditary!**

Babu comes out with a large tin of fresh Cashew nuts while the other lady softly ask her,

Lady 1: Hereditary diseases that we are unaware of !

The camera shifts to a close-up shot as the lady forcefully hammers a hard, burnt nut shell. With a loud crack, the shell breaks in half to reveal a pristine white cashew.

CHAPTER 57

A TERRIFIED 'KID'

Eve./Ext.

Manojan is sitting in his bedroom as a bad night falls, and he feels miserable. while Surabhi, sitting next to him, is deep in thought for a while before turning to him and looking deeply into his face.

Surabhi: If the father withdraws the case after they realise we're expecting kids, then everything might fall in place just like before, isn't it? That's the reason I...

With a strong suspicion Manojan looks at Surabhi while she continues,

Surabhi: Remember the day when you asked me not to take my lunch box? That noon I had shawarma from a local restaurant, maybe because of that I vomited that day. Other than that....

With much confusion, Manojan looks at Surabhi and asks her,

Manojan: That means, Surabhi?

Manojan puts his head down and slowly talks to Surabhi,

Manojan: Surabhi, I was about to lose the case against my dad if we have a baby. But now...

Surabhi hugs Manojan dearly while Manojan looks into to her eyes and continues,

Manojan: To be honest I was expecting our baby.., Surabhi

Surabhi: When everybody accuses you. I believe somewhere deep inside my Manojettan will never do that. Sorry.

Manojan: That's true, I used to hate and never liked children coming in front of me. But no one ever asked me the reason for my behaviour.

When I was a kid, Dad used to lock me up and hit me very badly for every small mistake I committed. I never know why he was so rude to me.

He has never been the way he is now. It might be due to his love and affection towards me he wanted me to always be right. As a kid then, it may have had a lasting impression on my soul this day I believe.

This is the after effects of the pain I suffered as a kid. If at all we have children, and if I tend to treat our children like my father did. I cannot tolerate that Surabhi..,

Manojan had tears in his eyes and was terribly hurt,

Surabhi: Nothing of that sort will happen I assure you Manojetta. Now don't feel sad thinking about that, okay? Just let it flow from your heart.

Manojan is emotional, The camera zooms in on Manojan's teary-eyed face as Surabhi embraces him. Surabhi is comforting him with a hug and tears in her eyes. The background music swells, adding to the emotional intensity of the scene.

CHAPTER 58

JOYS AND SORROWS

Montages

At present, Manojan's life is running down a nice parallel track of gratitude and pain. The camera shows a wide shot of Manojan's bike moving smoothly along the road with Surabhi sitting behind him, holding onto his waist. In the side mirror, we see Sonumon sitting in the backseat, his face full of excitement.

As they come to a stop in front of the school, the camera zooms in on Surabhi holding Sonumon's hand as they walk towards the entrance. The camera then cuts to a close-up shot of Manojan's face, his eyes filled with love for Sonumon as the bond grows stronger.

Manojan, out of love, every now and then finds some time to visit Sonumon at his house, plays with him, hugs him, and hands him a toffee. Sonumon is also very attached to Manojan, as he visits him every day with something or other.

And today was sports day, so Sonumon comes to Manojan's house and gives him the trophy he won as a gift, and Manoj's eyes light up with joy.

Manojan is very happy with Sonumon being so close to his heart. Days pass by as Manojan is busy with his pandal business and cashew nut export hand in hand, while Sumesh has been a great help in all his events, and Bengali Babu, as usual, pretending to be busy all the time, walks up and down the event doing nothing.

As his father approaches, Sonumon sprints. Sumesh, who can be seen hugging and embracing his son and smiling like a proud father, is close to Sonumon in particular; he meets him every day at his house with a pack of biscuits and a few colorful toffees.

It's clearly visible in his emotions and actions that Manojan likes kids these days and understands how important it is to have a child around.

CHAPTER 59

FLYING BALL

Day/Ext.

The camera pans out from a high drone shot, revealing the vast cricket ground surrounded by lush greenery. Children can be seen running around, playing cricket, while others are cheering and clapping from the sidelines. The distant sounds of laughter and joy can be heard.

Manojan stops his bike, picks up the ball flying towards him, and throws it back at the team. Captain Smijoy sees Manojan and asks the opposite team's captain, Diljith.

Smijoy: You can include Manojettan in your team.

Diljit: No way. If that person plays, the playing team will lose.

Manojan comes near the stump while Smijoy asks him.

Smijoy: Bro, do you want to join our team?

Manojan: If I bat, then I am in.

Manojan asks Diljit, who is running towards the bowling line, to bowl.

Manojan: Da..Is Purushettan at home?

Diljit prepares to bowl without responding, while Manojan takes the bat from Smijoy's grip and settles into the crease by pressing his legs tightly and hitting the bat to the ground.

Diljit aims and spins the ball towards Manojan's stumps. Manojan goes precisely, takes a step forward, and hits the ball with a perfect, powerful shot. Diljit, opening his mouth and looking up above, looks at the ball flying high in the air a few hundred meters away.

The ball rolls near Surabhi, who was walking along the road. Smijoy and his team members are happy while Diljith runs towards the stumps with a grumpy face. Manojan sees Surabhi, murmurs something to Smijoy, hands him the bat, and goes towards Surabhi

Manojan: Smijo, let me know if you are on the batting side. Okay.

Children watch Manojan run towards Surabhi. Shiju, the wicketkeeper, asks Diljit.

Shiju: Didn't you say that if he plays, the playing team will lose? What happened now?

Diljit: That's what I actually meant, the team against him shall lose, who played? We played? Who lost? We lost!

Shiju: You idiot mindbender. Get lost!

CHAPTER 60

'My World'

Eve./Int.

Sonumon's after-school routine seems to be visiting Manojmama at his house and playing with him. As usual, after all the fun, Manojan walks into Sumesh's house with Sonumon to drop him back. Suja comes out from the house to call him inside but Sonumon hugs Manojan tightly seeing Suja and tells,

Sonumon: Mano mama please come home tomorrow also, okay.

Manojan: Why not? Maman will come every day.

Sumesh walks out of the bathroom situated outside with a towel, wiping water trickling from his head.

Manojan: Sonumon doesn't seem to want me to go back.

Sumesh: Now, he can understand everything. He always takes your name and keeps remembering you.

Manojan: Yes Sumesh. Now I can feel all the love. I'm happy when I see how much you adore him and how much he loves you. But let me tell you one thing, never do anything out of your will and let him live his life.

And if you do that and restrict him with your dreams or ideologies he might one day revolt against you. Just like I did that to my father.

Manojan's eyes fill up, and he stutters out of words.

Sumesh: My son is alive today just because of you. Not just him, we too. He is My world. Don't be sad Manoja.

In the dim moonlight, the sound of crickets fills the air as Manojan slowly walks away. The stars twinkle above, and a lone owl hoots in the distance, his silhouette becoming smaller and smaller in the distance. Sumesh's expression is filled with concern and sadness as he watches his friend go. The darkness of the night seems to amplify the emotions of the moment.

CHAPTER 61

SURPRISES & MIRACLES

Montages

The camera captures the stunning view of the misty mountains as Manojan and Surabhi make their way up the winding path. Their faces are filled with hope and anticipation as they climb higher and higher, passing by other pilgrims on their journey. A duet song begins

"Climbing towards the heavens above

They hold hands with hope and love

A journey of faith, a journey of dreams

Their hearts are filled with hope...",

As they reach the top of the mountain, the camera pans out to show the magnificent temple, surrounded by the beautiful mist and clouds. Manojan and Surabhi stand in awe, looking up at the temple with reverence and gratitude.

The camera then cuts to a close-up of their faces, which are filled with emotions of joy and contentment.

Manojan and Surabhi are happy traveling around north Kerala and south Karnataka to many famous temples as they travel to Kundapura to try some local delicacies and enjoy the small gestures in life.

Manojan had sajjige rotti, a teatime snack, and coffee, while Surabhi had goli baje, a street food snack from Karnataka cuisine, served warm with coconut chutney. They shared a plate of buns, a deep-fried bread from the Udupi-Mangalore region.

Manojan and Surabhi are in Kollur Mookambika Temple, trying for some good fortune by sitting in front of the parrot astrologer while the parrot with its dark red beak pulls out a card from the cage. They both feel happy, with the card showing a child with a charming smile.

They enjoy these small moments and share the warmth of their relationship to the fullest when they arrive at Kannur Parassinikadavu, and they also pray at the Shashti Devi temple for children.

The camera pans over the lush green forests and coffee plantations of Coorg, near the border of Kerala and Karnataka. As the camera zooms in on a small resort nestled in the middle of the woods, we see Manojan and Surabhi sitting on the balcony of their room, gazing at the serene surroundings with contentment.

The camera then switches to a shot of them holding hands and walking along the winding paths of the resort, with the sun setting behind them.

The camera pans to the balcony, where the moonlight shines through the trees, casting a soft glow on Manojan and Surabhi lying in bed. Their bodies entwined as they gaze lovingly into each other's eyes. A gentle breeze rustles the curtains, and the sound of gentle music fills the room, adding to the romantic atmosphere.

They share sweet whispers and tender kisses, lost in the moment and the love they have for each other. The camera slowly zooms out as they hold each other, their bodies fitting perfectly together, and the scene ends with a romantic kiss as the camera fades to black, the song slowly drifts away, leaving behind a lingering track of emotions that will stay.

"With you by my side,

I feel like I can fly,

Let's take on the world,

One day at a time..."

Dissolve to

After visiting all of Kerala's and Karnataka's holy temples and places for a week, they return one fine day and visit Dr. Shanawa's and Dr. Shifali's clinic.

Manojan and Surabhi are sitting in front of the doctors with much excitement on their faces. Manojan is in the examination room.

Manojan looks at Surabhi with a mixture of sadness and love. She sobs helplessly. Manojan grips her hand tightly, wipes away her tears, and takes her hand in his. The doctor reminded both of them.

Dr. Shanawaz: Life is full of surprises and miracles...

CHAPTER 62

MEDICAL VERDICT

Day/Int.

On a bright and sunny day, Vijayan and Sumithramma ascend the stairs leading to William lawyer's office. They take a deep breath before reaching the top, where an elderly lady has just finished sweeping and mopping the floor to start the day.

They sit on the bench kept in front of his cabin while William lawyer comes in a hurry after some time surprisingly asks them,

William Lawyer: How come you both are here so early today? You could have just called me instead.

Vijayan and Sumitramma followed the lawyer as he entered the cabin. He looks at them, tired and tensed by their face he continues,

William Lawyer: Please Sitdown and tell me don't be tense.

He took a close look at both of their faces.

Vijayan: Lawyere..we are.. we want..to withdraw..

Lawyer: … Withdraw the case! What are you saying? Do you think we can withdraw a case so easily at this juncture? Do you think it is a child's game? to just do whatever you want and whenever you want?

William lawyer just looking terrible blown out after what Vijayan told him, looks at Sumithramma, and says

William lawyer: Sumithra yettaththiye, You are doing this without knowing the consequences. Didn't you and Vijayan sign that document? Didn't I warn you beforehand?

At the same time, William lawyer receives a message on Whatsapp. He checks the message and finds it's a message sent by Wilson lawyer.

He opens the file to see a medical report on Manojan. William Lawyer was clearly perplexed, with many different emotions on his face at once as he read the report.

William lawyer, with his eyes wide open and curving up his eyebrow, looks closely at both of their faces and says.

William Lawyer: Everything is upside down Vijaya, you will never win this case!

William Advocate shows them his mobile and continues

William Lawyer: If Wilson submits this medical report in the court, then everything will come to an end.

Vijayan: Lawyer, We didn't know about all this. We just came here to talk to you regarding the withdrawal of the case.

Lawyer: Then listen carefully, according to this report, Manojan will never have a child. Vijaya, do you remember what I said that day...if you bow down...

Vijayan is staring at Sumithramma. while the lawyer continues...

..they will run away with the nut. That's how the present generation are and our sons proved it.

After glancing at Sumithramma, Vijayan turns to face the lawyer.

CHAPTER 63

FINAL JUDGMENT

Day/Int.

As usual, the proceedings are yet to start inside the courtroom, and many lawyers and their clients are in the corridor walking towards the courtroom. After the court official calls out the official case number, the magistrate slowly opens and starts reading the case file. His facial expression hints at the final judgment as Manojan stands in the court hall. Wilson Lawyer comes to Manojan and says,

Wilson Lawyer: I created and whatsapp a fake medical report of yours to keep my father's mouth shut in court. He will never open his mouth hereafter.

Manojan nods his head. The Magistrate looks up at everyone present in the court hall and continues,

Magistrate: Hope everyone's present here?

William Lawyer: Yes your honour.

The camera cuts to a mid-shot of the magistrate as he looks at both lawyers with a smile.

Magistrate: Any good news?

Wilson Lawyer: No your honour.

Magistrate: Then, let me read out the final verdict. As per Succession Act 1956, this judiciary has decided that

Cheriyandiplackal Vijayan can decide to whom shall he pass on the inherited property.

Also as per constitution of India, Article 21, 14 & 19, just like a man or woman has the right to choose their partner, in the same way both the husband and the wife shall have all the right to decide if they want to have a kid or not. So the rest of what is said and appealed shall stay irrelevant, as per the law.

CHAPTER 64

Boy or a Girl

Night/Ext./Int.

Late at night, after the full moon shows up in the sky, As Manojan approaches the gate, the camera zooms in on his face, capturing the moon's unsettling glow and the weariness written across his features. Manojan slowly walks up, depressed and tired, and enters his room. Sumithramma comes after while he is taking off his shirt to go for a bath

Sumithramma: Manoja, Where have you been all day? Surabhi has been waiting for you since long, she hasn't had her dinner. She insisted on having it only after you returned home. Just go to her.

While Sumithramma still waits there talking to Manojan, Vijayan listening to them talking, slowly walks to them and in a low tone says,

Vijayan: Manoja... We did all this because we wanted to see our grandchild. I have nothing against you. I honestly desired what any grandparent on this earth might desire.

I felt, you should also have a child to support you in your older days, boy or girl. As you said, I know I have done something grave which no father should have done to his child.

As Vijayan stops talking, tears start to fall down his cheeks, and Manojan's eyes start to mist up as well. Seeing this Sumithramma too feels too emotional, with a brief silence wiping her eyes she says to Manojan

Sumithramma: You both stop crying like a kid now. Manoja, you go take a bath, and you both sit and eat. She's waiting for you, poor girl. We're going to bed. Let's get some sleep.

Dissolve to

Despite the fact that Surabhi was present and listening to all of these conversations, she had not said anything that might upset everyone's feelings.

As Manojan closes the door, the weight of all that has happened seems to finally hit him. Tears roll down his face, and he can't hold them back any longer. Surabhi, sensing his pain, gets up from the bed and walks over to him. She places a hand on his shoulder and softly wipes away his tears

Surabhi: Manojetta, what happened? In front of everyone... Why are you sad? finally you only won against everyone. Isn't it?

Manojan: Actually, We lost, isn't it, Surabhi?

Surabhi: Hey! Don't cry. We aren't the ones to decide everything. We haven't done anything wrong, have we? Don't cry.

Surabhi turns to him and embraces him tightly, his body shaking with sobs. Surabhi holds him close, whispering words of comfort and love. For a few moments, they stood there, wrapped in each other's arms. It's as if time has stopped.

As Manojan and Surabhi hold each other tightly, the camera slowly pans out and lifts up through the window, revealing the starry night sky. A gentle breeze rustles the curtains, as if signifying a new beginning.

As the camera continues to rise, the title "A Nutty Affair" appears on the screen, shimmering in the starlight. as an uplifting and emotional background song starts playing. The music lifts the mood and adds a sense of hope to the scene.

The scene gradually fades to black. It's the end of their story, but the beginning of a new chapter in their lives, marking the end of Manojan and Surabhi's journey, leaving the viewers with a sense of warmth and positivity, reminding them that even in the darkest of times, there is always hope.

The emotional music slowly fades away, leaving the viewers with a feeling of warmth and love in their hearts.

Fade in

CHAPTER 65

EPILOGUE

After 36 months

It's a bright, beautiful day, a drone shot captures an aerial view of the vast land surrounding Cheriyandi Plakkal House, slowly zooming in towards 'Manoj Events & Exports' at their 10 cent plot.

In the foreground, Vijayan and Babu are standing in front of the establishment. As the camera continues to move closer, Vijayan's old godown comes into view in the background.

Cut to a closer shot of Vijayan giving instructions to Babu, who stands obediently in front of him.

After a rattling sound caught his attention, Vijayan frantically looked around. A three-year-old toddler, toddling toward Vijayan from inside the house while holding a rattle in his tiny hand.

Vijayan's heart races as he watches the child slowly walk towards him, fear grips him, and he can feel his old phobia creeping up on him. In a panic, he raises his voice and shouts at the child to stop.

Surabhi... Surabhi... Sumithra... hey! Manoja.

The camera zooms in on Babu's face, his expression filled with doubt as he watches Vijayan and the child.

As the scene comes to an end, the screen fades to black and the words appear on the screen, displayed in typewriter format.

"Children don't owe us anything;

we owe them everything."

The words linger for a few moments before the credits begin to roll.

Hoping to be a motion picture soon.

www.ingramcontent.com/pod-product-compliance
Lightning Source LLC
LaVergne TN
LVHW050547160826
845677LV00011B/2216